This is my book

Teresa White

360 Kingsley St

San Diego Calif,

Phil laid the key beside Judy's plate.

"Mystery of the Jade Idol"   (See Page 33)

The Mystery Of The Jade Idol

by

Anna Andrews Barris

CUPPLES & LEON COMPANY
Publishers   New York

CONTENTS

MYSTERY BOOKS FOR GIRLS

THE JADE NECKLACE
by Pemberton Ginther

THE THIRTEENTH SPOON
by Pemberton Ginther

THE SECRET STAIR
by Pemberton Ginther

THE DOOR IN THE MOUNTAIN
by Izola L. Forrester

SECRET OF THE DARK HOUSE
by Frances Y. Young

THE TWIN RING MYSTERY
by Mildred A. Wirt

THE DORMITORY MYSTERY
by Alice Anson

MYSTERY OF THE LAUGHING MASK
by Mildred A. Wirt

ESCAPE BY NIGHT
by Alice Anson

and

THE MYSTERY OF THE JADE IDOL
by Anna A. Barris

CHAPTER I

THE JADE IDOL

IT WAS a dewy, fragrant morning in Mexico, too beautiful a day for the beginning of a mystery which was to mean suspicion, suffering, heartbreak and death. If Judy Winslow had known the outcome she never would have carried out the plan she had in mind.

An alarm clock went off in her bedroom in the Harrington plantation house. She slipped her hand through the opening in the mosquito netting canopy of her bed and silenced the buzzing noise. Then she lay there listening to the sounds in the patio below; the splashing of water in the fountain, the low chattering of Tito, the parrot, calling for something to eat, and the pat, pat of the cook making tortillas for the servants' breakfast.

Suddenly remembering why she had set the alarm for 5:30, she scrambled out of bed and hurried over to her cousin, Susanne Lawrence,

1

who was still sound sleep. With her pink and
white coloring and lovely blond hair, Susanne
looked like a sweet little girl much younger than
her seventeen years.

She was lying there so comfortably, Judy hesitated before wakening her, feeling guilty over
what she was planning to make Susanne do. She
wouldn't tell her until they were on the trail;
Susanne would object strenuously and think it
too risky. But Judy felt she could win her over.

She lifted the mosquito netting and gave
Susanne a little shake. "Hi there, honey, wake
up! It's a swell morning. Just right for a nice
long ride. Wake up, lazy bones."

For a second, Susanne looked at the tall, red
headed girl in green pajamas standing by her bed,
then closed her eyes again.

Judy patted Susanne's bare arm. "For heav-
en's sake, don't be so lazy. It's perfectly glorious
out. Come on, *darling*. If you keep on lying
there I'll yank you out of bed," she threatened.

Once awake, Susanne agreed it was a grand
morning and soon the girls were riding down the
trail straight into a mystery.

Judy, wearing an old pair of jodhpurs, looked
like a gay, young gypsy. Her vibrant hair was
tied with a green ribbon; a green, yellow and red
kerchief lay knotted about her throat. No such

attire for Susanne; she was very pretty and exceedingly chic in her custom made shirt, breeches and riding boots.

Now and then the girls waved friendly hands to the Indians who were picking bright red coffee berries and putting them into bags which swung from their shoulders. The men, women and children smiled at their two visitors from the States and called cheerily, "*Buenos dias, Señoritas! Buenos dias!*"

"Aren't they great, Susanne," Judy called back to her cousin. "Everything's swell down here; Aunt Alice, Uncle Jim, the darling rambling old plantation house, your horse and my beautiful, dapple-gray King. We're having one grand time." She pulled up her horse and waited for Susanne to come up beside her. "We're taking that other trail through the woods," she announced, trying to make her voice sound very casual. "It's so beautiful in there I know you'll enjoy it."

Susanne eyed her suspiciously. "Doesn't *that* trail lead to that old spooky building?"

Judy looked a bit sheepish. "Yes, it does. But you're not afraid to ride by that, are you?"

"Of course, I'm not afraid to ride *by* it," Susanne's voice was indignant. "But that's not what you're planning to do. You're going in. I told you before I won't do it, and I'm telling you again. Aunt Alice says it's so tumbled down it gives her the horrors just to look at it."

Judy did not meet Susanne's eyes. She was very busy brushing off a fly from King's satiny neck. "To tell the truth, I did think I might prowl around in that old abandoned monastery for a little while. Even if it is in ruins from an earthquake, it can't hurt us."

"Don't talk so silly. The ruins can't hurt us, but what's inside might. How do we know what's lurking in that old place? It really isn't safe for us to go by ourselves. Let's wait until José or someone can go with us. Please, Judy."

"And have a personally conducted tour!" Judy grunted. "A heap of fun we'd get out of that. Oh come on, Susanne. Don't be such a 'fraid cat.' "

She made a move as though to ride on. Susanne was weakening, but she sat still.

"It's haunted! That horrible place is haunted."

Judy pounced on the word "haunted." "That's the reason why it's safe for us to go in," she argued. "Uncle Jim told me that Indians are so superstitious he can't hire one to enter such a building. We shan't find a soul in there. And you'll love the ride through the woods. It's the most beautiful trail on the plantation, I'm going through that building this morning. You do as you please. Well, what have you decided?"

Susanne sighed. "All right. All right. You're getting your own way as usual. But this is the last time I'll give in to you," she warned. "We're always doing something so dangerous, I'll be a nervous wreck by the end of summer."

Judy turned her horse toward the other trail. "You're having a grand time and don't realize it," she laughed. "And this morning's going to be the best of all. You're a nice girl to follow your darling cousin." Judy turned around and smiled at her.

Susanne made a face. "I'm loony. That's what I am. The inside of my legs are still raw from the last time I followed you. That was a smart stunt for us to do, climbing those high trees."

Judy chuckled. "It was a smart stunt to hold a machete and climb clear to the top, then pry off an orchid plant with that huge knife."

Susanne's dimples began to show. "It was a stunt to get down, too. I'll bet I was fifty feet in the air. Whew, but I was dizzy. I'd be sitting on that limb yet, if you hadn't ridden to the plantation after those two Indians. Judy Winslow, you think of such crazy, wild things to do, no one would believe you came from Boston."

"Well anyone would know that you did," Judy laughed. "You're so afraid of doing things, you'd dry up and blow away, if you didn't have me around. Here we go now into the forest. You'll say too, it's one of the most beautiful places you've ever seen. Let's not ride fast, Susanne. I want to enjoy every bit of it."

The great trees were swathed and veiled in vines that blazed like emeralds under the enchantment of the sun. Yellow headed parrots with blue and red wings, flew across their path making a chattering noise. There were shy song birds and flaming macaws. Tiny, iridescent humming birds hovered for a moment over a flower, then darted out of sight.

"I told you it was lovely in here, Susanne. Aren't you glad you came?" Judy asked triumphantly.

Susanne was gazing at pinkish-lavender orchids, swaying on their slender stems, from great branches overhead.

"So lovely, it's like fairyland," she said softly. "Sorry orchids grow so high up in the trees. But just the same it's breath-taking to see them growing wild."

For nearly two miles, they rode in this magical forest. Then the trees became so close they darkened the trail; the branches bent low, and it was necessary to keep their heads down to avoid being hit.

"The way these woods have changed, I'll bet we're getting near that old haunted monastery," Susanne grunted, as she rubbed the back of her neck with her hand. "I've a cramp from all this ducking. How much farther do we have to go?"

Judy hadn't an idea. She had never ridden beyond the lovely section. All she knew was that this trail was supposed to lead to the monastery. "We've gone so far, we must be there pretty soon," she told her. "Cheer up, honey, I really believe we're almost there."

"Yes, cheer up, for we're about to see a nice, haunted—Judy, there it is! Look at it," Susanne gasped. "Oh my word. Look at it! Look at it!"

They rode on slowly toward a large stone building which was partly in ruins. From its moss-covered tower and walls, hung long, snake-like vines. Trees looked out of some of the windows, or stretched their dead branches like gray skeleton arms toward the sky.

Susanne edged her horse closer to Judy. "I never saw such a horrible place. Please, please, Judy, let's not go in."

Delightful thrills were going up Judy's spine. She had heard that the monastery was in ruins, but she had not expected anything so terrifying as this. "Not go in? Don't talk so crazily. I can hardly wait to get there."

Susanne said weakly, "I suppose, it is silly to be afraid of it, even though it does look so hideous. You don't believe in ghosts, do you, Judy? It's only silly talk about the monastery being haunted."

The Irish in Judy was saying, "Of course, there are such things." But the Scotch told her sternly, "Don't be ridiculous. You know better than that!"

The Irish was uppermost this morning. She was not telling Susanne, but she was hoping they might catch a glimpse of a banshee, or a specter in white. But all she said was, "Let's not talk about ghosts. Anyway, if there are such things, we wouldn't likely be seeing them in the day time. So don't worry about that. The trail's too narrow to ride side by side. Get Don Dexter behind me."

"All right. Whoa, Don. Whoa, boy." Susanne pulled on the reins, allowing Judy to get ahead. For a few minutes they rode along in silence. Then Susanne called in a low, frightened voice, "Judy, Judy, someone's coming! Listen!"

Pulling up their horses, they sat there listening

to the thud of hoofs which was becoming louder and louder.

"Perhaps it's Carlos, the superintendent, taking a short cut to Uncle's other plantation," Judy whispered. "I don't think there's anything to be afraid of."

Instead of Carlos, it was their handsome Uncle Jim Harrington and with him, a man they had never seen before.

When Susanne saw they were turning on the little path which led to the monastery, she went by Judy like a flash. "Uncle Jim!" she called. "Uncle Jim, please wait for us. We're going in there, too."

With hot, indignant eyes, Judy looked at the flying figure. Hadn't she told her she didn't want anyone to go with them! If Susanne had kept quiet they could have waited until the next day. Now they would be conducted through the monastery, the very thing she did not want. She realized there was nothing to do now but to make the best of it, so spurring King, she started after her.

"Thanks for waiting," Susanne exclaimed breathlessly, as she and Judy galloped up to the men. "I know it's silly, but I'm scared to go in. So I'm awfully relieved to have company. Whew, I'm hot," she laughed, as she mopped her perspiring, flushed face. "Don't believe I ever rode faster in my life."

There was no smile on their Uncle Jim's face. No annoyance. Only a look of not knowing what to do. He said quickly, "Good morning, Susanne. Good morning, Judy. Colonel Thompson, my two nieces from the States, Judy Winslow and Susanne Lawrence."

The girls were regarding Colonel Thompson with awe, for this gray haired man with the clipped mustache and skin as bronzed as an Indian, was the noted archaeologist who was uncovering an Aztec temple a few miles from there.

Susanne was ashamed she had rushed up to them. It was a rude, uncouth thing for her to do; her face flushed.

Judy was too thrilled over meeting this great man to think of anything else. If only he would invite them to visit the temple he was excavating. But if that never happened, it was enough just to meet this renowned archaeologist.

Colonel Thompson touched his sun helmet. "Good morning, Miss Susanne. Good morning, Miss Judy," he said gravely.

Then he gave Mr. Harrington a strange, questioning look. Susanne drew a quick breath. Judy, now as flushed as Susanne, said with a little smile, "It's wonderful to meet you, Colonel

Thompson. We'll run along now. Susanne's starved for her breakfast, so we'll wait until to-morrow to go through the monastery. Come on, Susanne. I'll race you home."

She was turning King with Susanne following, when Colonel Thompson stopped them.

"That's only an excuse Miss Judy. You're here now, so you girls might as well come with us," he said tersely.

Judy's face was scarlet. "Please don't feel you must invite us. We can come another time just as well."

The Colonel waved his riding crop impatiently, "No, no, come right along. We mustn't sit here and talk, but get inside where we can't be seen."

They followed the men, Susanne nervous, frightened; Judy all agog. Things were turning out to be quite thrilling after all.

They rode through a stone archway into the monastery courtyard, once beautiful, but now terrifying with its gnarled trees, broken fountain, and flowerbeds a tangle of weeds. A flagged walk led to an ancient sundial, and from a vine covered wall the stone face of a grotesque old man, laughed down at them. It too, had been a foun-tain, but for years, no water had flowed from its toothless, laughing mouth.

"What could their uncle and Colonel Thompson be coming here for," the girls wondered, "What secret thing could they be doing in this haunted place?"

The Colonel rode over to the stone balustrade of the cloister which surrounded the patio. "We'll tie our horses here," he said. Then went on in a low voice. "I discovered something yesterday, which your uncle has permitted me to bring here for safe keeping." He glanced around, then continued in a still lower voice, "It's a jade idol almost entirely covered with jewels."

Judy glanced around at the tumbled down building, "You're going to lock it up in here?" She wondered where he could possibly put it.

Uncle Jim was already off his horse, tying it to the balustrade. "Yes, he's going to lock it up in here, Judy. I have what I call my strong room. It'll be as safe in there as in a vault. Are you showing it to us, Colonel?"

"Of course I shall. Think of it, Susanne and Judy; this idol lay under that Aztec temple altar for more than a thousand years. I'll show it to you, and you'll understand what a rare thing I've found."

The girls were almost in a daze as they got off their horses, tied them to the balustrade, and went up the moss covered steps of the cloister.

Susanne stumbled over a broken tile, as she watched a green lizard scurry behind one of the stone columns.

Judy grabbed her arm, "Look where you're going, Susanne! Do you want to break your neck?"

"I'll be careful." Susanne limped a few steps. "Glory, I certainly wouldn't want to break my neck in a spooky old place like this."

The men were waiting for them before a door on which was a huge padlock. Their uncle took a key from a pocket in his breeches, and called their attention to the heavy, iron staples. "I want you to notice how strong these are. And when you get inside, you will see how very much like a vault the room is. The walls are five feet thick, and there are stone bars across the windows. It's absolutely impossible for anyone to break in here. So don't worry, Judy, the idol will be perfectly safe in this room of mine."

"It should be," Judy agreed. "My goodness, this looks as strong as a fortress. I didn't dream you had any room like this in this old wreck of a monastery."

"Please move over a bit, Susanne, while I get this unlocked. Thanks." Jim Harrington inserted the flat, brass key, turned it, pulled the lock out of the staples and pushed open the heavy oak door. "Go on in," he said to the girls, "and don't look so frightened, Susanne. The Colonel's directly behind you."

"I'm not scared, Uncle Jim," Susanne said in a low voice. "I'm only excited, that's all."

They entered a cool, dim room with high vaulted ceiling and great rafters. Judy was looking about her in amazement. "Why Uncle Jim, this is a chapel. It's not like a fortress at all. It's lovely."

Light filtered through vine-covered, narrow windows set high in the stone wall. At one end of the room was an altar, and in a deep recess, stood a hollowed stone baptismal font, about four feet high. To the right of the altar was a door, across which was a heavy iron bar.

The Colonel laid the saddlebag on a long table, which years ago had been brought in from the refectory. They gathered around and watched with bated breath, as he unfastened the straps and lifted out an object two feet long, swathed in a strip of white cotton cloth. Very slowly, very carefully, he removed the covering and held up before them a gorgeous, glittering, hideous green idol.

The girls stared at its protruding eyes of yellow stones, and mouth, cruel with sharp fangs; golden serpents were twined about its fat, green body, and it was wearing a gold necklace of jewel incrusted heads and hearts.

A low gasp from Judy was the only sound. It was Susanne, who found her voice first. "His eyes are terrible. They're looking at me as though they're alive," she whispered.

Judy said in a low, trembling voice, "Don't talk so silly. It isn't alive. The idol's only a piece of jade."

"His eyes aren't very loving, that's a fact, Susanne," her Uncle Jim said. "But child, how can you expect a War God to have kind eyes. This is a War God, isn't that so, Colonel?"

"Yes, it's Huitzilopochtli, the great War God of the Aztecs, the most feared and powerful god they had. And this is the most magnificent I've ever seen. Look at the jewels in the necklace, and see how the heads of the snakes and the full length of their bodies are covered with topaz and emeralds." The Colonel was slowly turning it around, so they might see its entire beauty. "Gorgeous, isn't it? Gorgeous!"

Susanne had backed away. But Judy was fascinated. She wanted to touch it, to feel the shiny, smooth green body, the sparkling topaz and emeralds.

The Colonel was taking the long strip of white

cloth from the table. Here was her chance. She said eagerly, "Please let me hold the idol while you wrap it up. Please, Colonel Thompson, give it to me? I'll hold it for you."

But her uncle said quickly, "No, no, don't give it to her, Thompson. You're so excited, Judy, you might let it drop. And it's heavier than you think, dear. I'll help you, Thompson."

Judy was disappointed. But she said with a little laugh, "Perhaps it's just as well you're holding it, Uncle Jim. I am terribly excited. Thank you so much, Colonel Thompson for showing the idol to me. I'll never forget this gorgeous thing as long as I live. Wouldn't it be a tragedy if anyone should steal it!"

"Indeed it would," the Colonel turned the idol a bit, so Mr. Harrington could get the cloth under the left arm of the god. "A few months ago, a jeweled knife disappeared before I could take it to Mexico City. So I'm asking you and Susanne to keep the finding of this a secret. Only my two assistants, and two Indians who were with me, when it was uncovered, know anything about it. I have sworn them to secrecy. However, it is impossible to be sure of anything down here. A great many people would be unscrupulous enough to steal it for the price they could get for the jewels."

When it was again wrapped up, he held open the saddlebag while Mr. Harrington very carefully laid the idol inside. Then he stood there looking around the room. "Let me see. I'll carry it over to that dark corner. It would be exactly as safe here," he said with a little smile, "but naturally, a dark corner seems a more fitting place to hide things."

Their uncle said, "Colonel don't let me forget to give you the key, for I'm leaving immediately for my other plantation and shall be gone for two weeks. To be on the safe side, you'd better take one of my Indians as a guard."

Colonel Thompson turned, a worried look on his face.

"By George, I had forgotten about that! Didn't think I'd need a bodyguard on my way home. No one knows for certain that I brought the idol over here, but as I have used this place before they *might* surmise. I hope no one holds me up and steals the key."

"Colonel Thompson, please let me keep it for you?" Judy asked eagerly. "I'll take good care of it."

He seemed startled at her suggestion and almost curtly declined.

But Judy would not take "No" for an answer. Not only was she eager to do a kindness for the

Colonel, but she wanted the thrill of having charge of such a priceless treasure.

Susanne would not have dared to keep on teasing the dignified and rather austere Colonel. But not Judy. It had never occurred to her to have fear of anyone. She continued to plead.

"Where would you keep the key?" her uncle asked, feeling quite disturbed over Judy's persistence. "What would you do with it if Colonel Thompson did permit you to take it?"

"Oh I'll hide it—" She wrinkled up her forehead and thought hard. Her face brightened. "I know. I'll slip it in the toe of one of my blue pumps. No one would think of looking in there."

The Colonel could see that Judy was a very determined young lady. She was also impulsive and he was afraid, a bit unreliable. Like her uncle, he was not very much pleased with her persistence. Judy kept on, until at last, very reluctantly, the Colonel told her she might have charge of the key.

They were two very thrilled girls who a little later mounted their horses, said good-bye to the men and went galloping down the trail to the house.

Judy could scarcely wait to tell her Aunt Alice about the idol and that she, Judy Winslow was

in charge of this priceless treasure. She felt her
aunt would be thrilled and proud of her.

Susanne called, "Hi, Judy! Just made up a
song about you. Listen! Galloping along, she
kept time with her riding crop as she sang lustily,

> "*J stands for Judy,*
> *I know she is loony,*
> *For she thinks up such crazy things to do.*
> *She scares me so completely*
> *My bones shake creakily.*
> *If she doesn't reform, she'll rue!*"

"I'm loony, am I? Just the same you had a
good time this morning. If I hadn't made you
go to the monastery you wouldn't have seen the
idol. You'd better thank me for that, Susanne
Lawrence."

Susanne stopped her fooling. "I really do
thank you, Judy. But I'm certainly happy to be
out of that old, spooky temple and away from the
idol. I never want to lay eyes on that frightful
War God again."

"Well don't worry, no one's going to show it
to you," Judy said. She was thinking Susanne
would hate the idol all the more if she happened
to think of the sacrificial stone they had seen in
the National Museum in Mexico City. On this

stone Aztec priests had sacrificed hundreds of human lives as an offering to the War God. They had seen too, sacrificial knives the priests had used.

Judy shuddered as she thought of the men, women and children who had been sacrificed before this jade god now in the monastery. It was very evident Susanne had not thought of the idol in connection with human sacrifice, for she would have spoken of it. Susanne was scared enough of the idol now, and Judy wasn't telling her anything to make her more afraid.

When they rode into the patio Susanne gave a happy sigh. "Look at the fountain splashing into its basin; see the flowers, the orange trees and our breakfast table under the rose arbor. This is some contrast to that gloomy old place we just left. Oh boy, am I glad to be here!"

"I feel better myself," Judy admitted. "But just the same I wouldn't have missed this morning for a million dollars. Where on earth is Pedro!"

She clapped her hands three times. An old Indian, sandalfooted, his shirt flopping outside his cotton trousers, came hurrying in from the back courtyard to take their horses.

Rosetta, their fat old housekeeper, also appeared. She came waddling down the path holding a sheet of paper and there was a worried expression on her usually placid face. Judy slid off King. "What's that, Rosetta?" she asked anxiously. "Is it a note for us?"

"Si, a letter it is for you Señoritas. The Señora has gone."

"Aunt Alice gone!" Judy gasped. "Oh Susanne, what do you suppose has happened?" In a second, Susanne was off her horse, and the two girls were reading;

"My dear Girls:
This morning I received a telephone message that my friend Mary Watson is seriously ill. She lives on a plantation fifty miles away, and as the trail is so rough one can go only on horseback, I am leaving at once, in order to get there as soon as possible.

Her sister is expected to arrive from the States either tomorrow, or the next day. I shall stay until she comes.

Oh my dears, I am so troubled over leaving you alone, I am almost beside myself. Rosetta and Pedro have promised to take good care of you, but they are only servants and would not presume to dictate. I am begging you to ask their advice before doing anything out of the ordinary. And please, please, do not go off the plantation without taking Pedro with you.

I shall call you tonight on the telephone.

> Your very much worried
>
> Aunt Alice."

Judy stared at the signature. They were alone on the plantation. It would have given her a queer feeling at any time, but now with the jade idol in her care, their unexpected isolation left her stunned.

CHAPTER II

Susanne was saying, "Oh Judy, I don't like to have Uncle Jim and Aunt Alice so far away. I don't like it one bit."

She looked so frightened, Judy said with a bravado she was far from feeling, "What if Uncle Jim and Aunt Alice aren't here! We're not alone when more than two hundred Indians are picking coffee on the place, and with Rosetta, Marie, Pedro and the other servants in the house. I'm surprised at you!"

"I didn't say there aren't Indians here," Susanne told her. "It wouldn't make any difference if there were a million; we'd still be the only white people. I'm scared. Good and scared. You'd own up too, if you weren't ashamed."

Judy was not owning up. She patted the green, yellow and red kerchief knotted around her neck. "See this?" she asked, smiling broadly. "Every time I wear this gay thing it brings me good luck. I had it on when I took my exams. I was wearing it when I received the letter from Aunt Alice inviting me down here. And didn't I have it on this morning when I took the key? We'll have the time of our lives staying here alone. I just thought of something exciting; we may have our names in the papers. How's this for a swell headline, 'TWO AMERICAN GIRLS GUARD JEWELED IDOL?' Wouldn't that be something? Wouldn't it?"

They eyed each other. Susanne admiringly, Judy, a bit uneasily. Susanne said, "You little fibber! You're not fooling me. You're as scared as I am. But you're too game to let on. Own up, Judy. Come on, own up."

Judy's face was grave. "I'm not exactly frightened," she said slowly. "But of course, I'd rather have Aunt Alice and Uncle Jim here. Susanne, remember this, being afraid doesn't help anything. And talking about it makes things seem worse. We're not going to act like cowards. We weren't brought up that way."

Susanne flushed. "I know it, Judy. I'm ashamed of myself." She said in a voice as sweet as honey, "If I promise not to show the yellow streak again, will you still like me?" She held up her face. "Kiss me and tell me you will. Hurry! Kiss me!"

Judy laughed as she leaned down and kissed Susanne on her soft, pink cheek. "You're a

darling if you are a scared cat. I'd love you if
you showed the yellow streak a thousand times.
Now, after settling that important question, let
me see if my precious key is still here." She
thrust her hand into the pocket of her jodhpurs.
"Yes, here it is," she laughed. "I'll not hide it
in my blue slipper until after breakfast. I'm
starved." She threw her gloves on a chair and
started across the courtyard. "Come on, honey."

"Wait a minute," Susanne said in a low voice.
She was looking at a pretty, black-eyed maid who
was placing a dish of fruit on the breakfast table.
"I hope Marie doesn't find out we have the key,
or that the idol is in the monastery. She's as
flighty as she's pretty, and I don't trust her one
bit."

Judy said she felt the same way about Marie,
but that no one would find out a thing if they
kept still. They must do that. They must not
tell a soul.

They were eating their grapefruit and Marie
was bringing the coffee, when they noticed that
the maid was smiling at someone across the patio.

A tousle haired, dark-eyed boy, wearing a blue
shirt open at the throat and an old pair of
breeches and boots, had ridden into the courtyard and was coming slowly down the driveway.

He looked so astonished, Susanne giggled. "Hope he doesn't tumble off from the shock of seeing us," she whispered.

Judy poked her under the table. "Keep still, Susanne. He'll hear you."

Susanne refused to keep still. She went on wickedly, "He's eyeing you, Judy. I bet he's wondering where that queer looking red head came from."

"Hello—I mean, good morning! Didn't know Mrs. Harrington had company," he stammered, pulling up his handsome dapple-gray horse.

"Good morning," Susanne's blue eyes were twinkling. "Yes, Aunt Alice has company. This is Judy Winslow and I'm Susanne Lawrence. We're spending the summer down here."

"You're spending the summer!" He beamed delightedly. "Jiminity, two girls from the States way down here in Mexico! Can't believe you're real. I'm Phil Stanton of the next plantation. I visited in Cleveland after Commencement and only got here last night."

They had surmised who he was. Aunt Alice had told them about the tall, good looking Phil Stanton who lived on the adjoining place. They knew he rode like an Indian, played tennis, swam and was a good dancer. They had been hoping he would arrive soon.

"We thought you were Phil Stanton," Susanne told him. "You see Aunt Alice has told us a lot about you. We've been looking for you for over a week."

"You have? Gosh, that makes me feel swell. If I'd known you girls were here I'd have cut my visit short." He went on with a broad grin, "Two girls from the States way down here. Oh boy, I can't believe it yet!"

"Well, we are here and we're eating breakfast. Won't you have some with us?" Judy asked. "We'd like to have you."

Phil slid off his saddle so quickly the girls laughed. "Sure, I will. Was afraid you weren't going to ask me." He threw the reins across a rose bush, went over to the table and sat across from Judy.

"Hi, Marie. It's nice to see you again," he said, smiling up at the pretty maid.

"Gracias, Felipe. Gracias." And Marie, all smiles, commenced to serve him.

"Why aren't you all excited this morning?" Phil asked, unfolding his napkin. "You're sitting here as calm as anything."

"Why should we be excited?" Judy wanted to know. "We're awfully thrilled to see you, but we're not terribly excited."

Phil looked up from sprinkling sugar on his

grapefruit. "Say, stop kidding me. You know well enough I'm not such an idiot as to believe you'd get excited over me. I was talking about the idol."

The smile left Judy's face.

"What idol?"

Phil put the spoon back in the sugar bowl and stared at the girls. "Do you mean to say you don't know your uncle has an idol locked in the monastery? That Colonel Thompson found one all covered with jewels and brought it over this morning to what your uncle calls his strong room?"

There was silence for a moment.

"Who told you?" Susanne asked.

"Francisco, one of our Indians. He was Marie's best beau when I went away. How about it, Marie?" He did not wait for an answer, but went on enthusiastically, "Last night, he told me that it had been discovered, and this morning saw Colonel Thompson riding over here. As the Colonel has used this room before, Francisco put two and two together. So I came over hot foot to get Mr. Harrington to show it to me. You must see it, too. Why they say it's covered with jewels from top to bottom! Won't that be something to see!"

Marie's black eyes were glowing. Carefully filling Phil's cup with coffee and hot milk, she said in her soft, rich voice, "So the idol is here, Felipe. I am very glad."

Judy straightened. "Go to the kitchen at once and bring more rolls, Marie. Go right along," she said sharply. "Go on!"

When the girl had disappeared, Judy admitted slowly, "We knew about the idol, but were hoping to keep it a secret. I'm dreadfully sorry Marie heard you."

Phil leaned back in his chair overwhelmed with what he had done. "Gosh, I hadn't an idea it was a secret. Gee, but I'm sorry."

He was so distressed, Susanne said quickly, "Don't feel so badly. How on earth would you know we wanted to keep it quiet. It's perfectly all right that you said that in front of Marie."

Phil ran his hand savagely through his hair. "No, it isn't all right. If you didn't want it told, I had no business to tell it. I'll bet you wish I hadn't come."

"Of course not," Judy told him. "We're really awfully glad you're here. Other people know about it, so I suppose Marie would find it out anyway." Her thoughts flew to Francisco. It didn't seem possible he could know the idol was in the monastery. "Colonel Thompson never found it until late yesterday afternoon. How on earth did the news get around so soon?" she asked in dismay.

Phil shrugged his shoulders. "Search me! But a thing can happen thirty miles from the plantation and in less than an hour the Indians will know all about it. Dad calls it jungle telegraphy."

Susanne told him they had seen the idol; that she and Judy were with their Uncle Jim when Colonel Thompson put it in the strong room. "Phil Stanton you can't imagine how gorgeous it is!" she said enthusiastically. "But you should see his eyes. They're yellow and stare right through you. Whew, he made my blood run cold."

Phil laughed. "He's only a piece of jade, so he can't eat you up, even if his eyes are fierce. But say, he must be a corker. Soon as I finish I'm going to hunt up your uncle and get a look at the old duffer myself."

Judy said quietly, "Uncle Jim isn't here. He left this morning for his other plantation and will be away for two weeks."

Phil said gloomily, "Isn't that my rotten luck. I bet he gave the key to Colonel Thompson." Suddenly, his face brightened. "He couldn't have left the key with your aunt, could he?" In his excitement over seeing the girls he had not thought about her absence. Now he asked anxiously, "Where is Mrs. Harrington? I hope she isn't sick."

"No, she's gone over to Mrs. Watson's," Judy said, and then told him of the message their aunt had received that morning. "So you see, with Aunt Alice and Uncle Jim both away, it's rather upsetting to learn so many people know about the idol. We feel responsible."

Phil looked amazed. "Responsible? What in heck are you talking like that for? Even if your aunt and uncle were here they wouldn't be sitting outside the monastery guarding the idol." He grinned at them. "I can tell you one thing you won't need to worry about. No Indian's going to break in there. They think the monastery's haunted. I know for sure it is."

Judy's eyes were twinkling, "Like fun you do. Don't try to tell us a silly thing like that. How do you know?"

"Because I heard a strange noise and saw a light in there one night when I was going by. Did I beat it! Gosh, you couldn't see me or my horse for the dust!"

The girls laughed and Judy told him she didn't believe a word of it.

Phil insisted he had told the truth. He went on seriously, "I don't believe in ghosts either. But I did see a light and hear a queer noise in the monastery last summer when I was home." He went on eagerly, "Let's look for the key. Maybe Colonel Thompson didn't take it after all. Your Uncle Jim wouldn't care if I found it. He's let me look at things in his strong room hundreds of times. I'd know that little old key anywhere. It's brass and about this size," he said, measuring with his hands, "and it has a heart shaped handle. Because there are a couple around here nearly like it your Aunt Alice has marked it with a red string."

Susanne's blue eyes were beseeching Judy to show him the idol.

Judy was saying fiercely to herself, "They know the War God is in the monastery, but I'd like anyone to find out who has the key! I'm not trusting anyone."

She helped herself to another biscuit and smiled at the boy sitting opposite her.

"Let's not talk any more about that old thing. Wouldn't you like to go swimming? I'll hunt up one of Uncle Jim's bathing trunks, and—" She was making grimaces trying to stop a sneeze. It was too late. "Ker-ch-ew!" she went loudly. "Ker-cheew!"

Wildly, she felt for her handkerchief, yanked it out of her pocket and with it came the key.

Susanne, Marie and Phil saw it fly over on the path, only Judy, who was holding the handkerchief to her nose and laughing, was unaware of what had happened.

Phil walked over, picked it up, held it for a moment, then without a change of expression, laid it on the table beside Judy's plate.

"What's that?" she asked. When she saw the key her face grew flaming red. "Oh," she gasped, "it belongs to—my trunk. I pulled it out of my pocket, did I? Thanks, a lot."

She didn't know Phil was thinking, "For Pete sake, the little devil had it all the time! Why in heck is she keeping it a secret?" It occurred to him that she might have promised not to tell anyone. Well, it was okay with him. He wouldn't make a row over it. He'd see the idol anyway, for when their uncle came he'd show it to him. He said to them, "I guess you think I'm a nut. I was so crazy to see the idol that's all I talked about. Don't even know what states you girls are from. From now on, I'm going to talk about you. And sure, I'll go swimming."

Up in their room getting ready, Susanne was scolding Judy. "Look at you," she stormed, "throwing that key on the bed. You'll forget and leave it there. That's how careless you are."

Judy was pulling off her jodhpurs. "Had to take it out of my pocket, didn't I? Before we leave I'll hide it in my blue slipper, so don't have a fit, grandma."

Susanne was getting out of the closet her red and white bathing suit and Judy's green one. She kept on scolding, "If Colonel Thompson knew how irresponsible you are he'd never given you the key. See what you did today. You pulled it out of your pocket with your handkerchief and wouldn't have known what happened to it, if we hadn't seen it fall on the path. And another thing; Phil knew that key. He must have a swell opinion of us."

Judy said calmly, "Oh he didn't recognize it. I was scared stiff when I saw it by my plate, but when he kept still I knew he hadn't sensed what it was. So get that off your mind, Susanne."

Seeing Judy's blue slippers on the closet floor Susanne leaned down picked one up, walked across the room and thrust it in Judy's hand. "You put that key in here this minute, Judy Winslow," she ordered. "We don't want to worry about it anymore. Hurry, put it in!"

Judy's face dimpled. "Instead of putting it in this darling blue slipper, I guess I'll wear it on a chain about my neck. It'll make a swell pendant."

Susanne threw her the key. "Put the key in the slipper and quit your fooling. Please, Judy—"

There was a slight noise out in the hall. Both turned and noticed that the door was slightly open. Judy went over and looked outside, but saw no one.

Susanne said firmly, "I certainly heard someone. Whoever it was must have gone down stairs."

Judy began to laugh. "What idiots we are. We forgot Phil was dressing in Uncle Jim's room. Of course, that's who it was. Well, whoever it was couldn't have heard us talking about the blue slipper for we weren't speaking loudly at all."

There was no more fooling. The slipper, with the key inside was placed beside its mate in the closet; quickly the girls got into their bathing suits and hurried down to their guest.

They had the cook pack a lunch, then went up river in a canoe to Phil's favorite swimming hole. The girls had a fine day with their new acquaintance, but 36 hours later, they would have given anything if they had never met Phil Stanton.

After he had gone; after they had supper and

telephoned their aunt, not telling her a word about the idol or the key, they stood in the doorway of the living room looking out on the moonlit patio.

It was a silver and black night, with a full moon and soft, twinkling stars. The splashing water of the fountain had turned to silver, and over all was the heady perfume of orange blossoms and masses of oleander.

The night before Susanne had been in raptures over the tropical moon, but now she said in a voice not quite steady, "It certainly looks ghostly out there, doesn't it?"

Judy was peering intently at something that was moving over by the wall. She drew a deep breath of relief when she realized it was only the grotesque shadows made by the swaying leaves of a palm tree. It was silly to be nervous.

She realized that they would become panicky if they did not get their minds on something else. "There's nothing out there to be afraid of," she said. "It's beautiful, Susanne. Just as lovely as it was last night and the night before that, ever since we've had full moon. I'll get my guitar and have some music. It'll be a lot of fun singing under that orange tree."

Susanne drew back. "Oh no, I can't go out

there. I simply can't. Well, I might, if you hunt up Pedro," she said reluctantly, feeling Judy would be disappointed were she to refuse.

Judy gave a nervous, little laugh. "Of course, we'll have him. We must have an audience, mustn't we?"

She played Mexico's love music, and soon, not only Pedro, Rosetta, José and the other house servants, but many coffee pickers were standing in the patio listening to the songs of the girls.

"Look who's coming!" Judy laughed. "See Marie with a brand new beau."

Marie was wearing a very full, gaily sprigged cotton skirt, a bright waist and flowers in her dusky hair. She was laughing and talking and showing her pleasure that she had made a conquest of the strange, handsome Indian she had in tow.

With his pink shirt open at the throat, golden brown sash holding his white cotton trousers and enormous sombrero perched jauntily on his head, this flashing-eyed young fellow not only was handsome, but picturesque.

"He looks like a movie actor," Susanne whispered.

He was so resplendent, so spectacular, Judy stopped her singing, only thrummed her guitar and watched as the two sauntered across the patio. They came quite near to the girls, and for awhile, stood there listening to the music.

Suddenly, Marie began to dance. Susanne sprang to her feet. "You're wonderful, Marie! You're perfectly wonderful! Oh I wish I could dance like that."

Marie slipped her long, red silk scarf (rebosa) from her shoulders. Whirling it high, she pirouetted and danced and stamped her dainty little feet, giving a colorful portrayal of one of the most popular Spanish dances. All at once she stopped, threw kisses to her applauding audience, then laughing, ran out of the courtyard, with her Indian in close pursuit.

"Pedro, who is that fellow?" Judy asked.

Pedro shrugged his thin shoulders. "He Ricardo. Come from up river." He jerked his thumb northward and made a grimace.

"Why Pedro, what a look on your face," Judy teased. "He's very handsome. Don't you like handsome men?"

"He no good," Pedro said gruffly. "I say he no good."

"Why Pedro, you don't know him, do you?"

"I don't know him. But he no good," Pedro insisted. "That fellow has a bad eye."

Judy laughed. She felt old Pedro did not approve of this stranger, because the Indian was dressed a bit too elaborately.

They sang until after eleven o'clock. On their way up stairs, Susanne said ruefully, "I don't know what Aunt Alice would say if she knew we stayed up until midnight, but it's still too gorgeous to go in." She put her arm across Judy's shoulders. "Listen, honey, I want you to show Phil the idol when he comes tomorrow. We both know he recognized that key. He couldn't help it, for he had just finished describing it, ribbon and all, when you pulled it out of your pocket. He's been such a good sport for not letting on, you should show it to him."

Judy agreed that Susanne was right; he couldn't have helped but recognize it. "And he certainly has been swell," she said. "As soon as he comes in the morning we'll take him down to the monastery. He deserves that and more too for being so nice after we acted as though we didn't trust him." She yawned. "I'm sleepy. We'd better hustle to bed for we promised to go riding with him at eight o'clock."

It was a little after two when Susanne was wakened by a noise. She lay there listening. The moon had gone down so the room was quite dark, but she could see the outline of someone near the closet.

Thinking it was Judy and wondering what she was doing up this time of night, she asked anxiously, "What's wrong, Judy? Are you ill?"

There was no answer.

"Didn't you hear me Judy? Are you ill?" she repeated, lifting the mosquito netting canopy and scrambling to the floor.

Judy mumbled half asleep, "What do you want, Susanne?"

Judy was in bed! Susanne's hand flew to her throat. That person over by the closet wasn't Judy! She could now see that it was a man who was standing over there. Her eyes were wide with terror as she gave one startled cry after another.

The fellow started for her. Screaming, Susanne got into bed and threw herself face downward.

The man kept on coming, and Judy too, was now screaming. Evidently afraid of the noise, the fellow shouted a curse at them, then turned, raced across the room and jumped through the open window to the upstairs porch.

With trembling fingers Judy switched on the light, slid to the floor and hurried over to her hysterical cousin.

"He's gone. I heard the vines tear as he went down the post. He can't hurt us, for he's gone.

Please stop crying." She leaned down, patted the girl. "Oh Susanne, please stop."

Susanne sat up and rubbing the back of her hand across her eyes she sobbed, "Oh Judy, I thought he was going to kill me. I thought he was going to kill me. He frightened me, so I—"

A terrifying thought had suddenly come to Judy. She turned and looked at the closet. The door was open! She went tearing across the room crying, "I'm afraid he was after the key! I bet that's what he was after, Susanne. Oh I'm afraid he's stolen the key!"

Her blue slippers were not in their accustomed place. Even though she knew she had placed them way back in the closet against the wall, frantically she pawed through their other shoes, trying to find them. But the blue slippers were gone.

CHAPTER III

"DO NOT TOUCH THE WAR GOD"

"HE'S TAKEN the key, Susanne! He's stolen the key!" Judy raced over to the window calling wildly for Pedro, José and Rosetta.

In a minute, Susanne was with her. "There is the thief!" she whispered. "Down there by the post." She pointed across the courtyard. "See him, Judy? See him?"

"Oh yes, I see him. Oh—there he goes!"

The man sprinted down the long corridor with the speed of a deer, passed the kitchen, turned back and darted through the open door.

The girls kept calling for Pedro and the other servants. It only was a matter of minutes, but it seemed ages until Pedro with José at his heels came running in from the back courtyard.

Judy shouted, "A thief's gone into the kitchen! Hurry, Pedro! Hurry!"

The men disappeared through the open doorway.

Rosetta came hurrying into the room almost

beside herself with fear for the girls. "Was the
thief in here?" she asked. "Was he in this
room?" She put her arm around Susanne who
was now crying. "Did he hurt you, Señorita?
Oh my little dear, did he hurt you?"

"No, no he didn't hurt me, Rosetta. . . . I'm
only nervous. . . . He frightened me terribly. . . . I was so frightened . . . so frightened."

Rosetta held her close. "You cry, Señorita.
You cry hard if you want to. You poor frightened little girl."

Judy was standing at the window watching for
the return of the men. She said, "Marie is frightened too. Look at her leaning against the archway of the back patio afraid to come in. It's
after two o'clock and she hasn't been to bed yet,
for she's still wearing that pretty dress of hers."

Rosetta scowled and muttered something
about Marie staying up so late with that no good
Ricardo. Then, calling on all the saints to help
Pedro and José catch the thief, she hustled the
girls down stairs, where like Marie, they watched
the door through which the men had disappeared.

In a short while Pedro and José returned out
of breath. Pedro told them that the thief had

run out the back door and climbed the high stone wall of the courtyard. They had chased after him, but the fellow had made his escape.

The thief had eluded them. The full meaning of this came to Judy. The man would be on his way to the strong room to get the idol.

"Oh Pedro, go to the monastery as fast as you can. The thief's after the idol. Hurry, Pedro," she cried desperately. "Hurry! Hurry!"

Pedro did not move. He squinted at her incredulously. "The idol? The thief is after the idol?"

Judy grabbed his arm. "Yes, the key was in our room. He stole it, Pedro. Don't you understand? The thief's trying to get the jade idol that's locked in the strong room. Hurry, Pedro. Don't stand there looking at me like that. Hurry, Pedro! Hurry!"

Pedro started across the courtyard on a run. "Get your machete, José! I get my gun. We catch that fellow. We catch him."

Judy sank on the steps and buried her face in her arms. "Why did I ask for the key," she sobbed. "What will Colonel Thompson say? Oh I wish I were dead. I wish I were dead."

Susanne realized full well how Judy was feeling. But it was not sympathy she needed now, but a bracing up. "How could you help that man coming into our room and stealing the key? Stop acting like a baby. I'm ashamed of you." She pulled a handkerchief from her pajama pocket and thrust it into Judy's tightly clinched hand. "Here, wipe your eyes and sit up like a sensible girl. Come on, Judy, sit up."

Judy did not sob any longer, but her face was still buried in her arms. In spite of Susanne's comforting words she knew she had asked for the key. She also realized that no one would have known where it was if she had put it in her slipper as soon as she had come upstairs, instead of throwing it on the bed. And besides that, she had fooled about it; had talked and talked about her blue slipper, while all the time, someone was listening. "A smart person she was!"

Susanne walked over to a green parrot who was pacing nervously back and forth on his perch under an orange tree. "Poor Tito, did we awaken you? I'm sorry. That's right, put your head down and I'll scratch it for you."

As she stood there scratching the yellow spot on Tito's head fear gripped her. What if Pedro or José should be killed in their fight with the thief? Dear old Pedro was such a devoted servant he would willingly give up his life for any member of the family, or to protect anything they valued. She and Judy might have been murdered! She wished the old idol never had been discovered.

It was a grueling, long wait until José returned. Pedro was staying at the monastery until daylight, then José would go back and take his place. The *Señoritas* were not to worry, for as long as the idol was in the strong room someone would guard the door.

When at last, the girls went upstairs, they were grateful for Rosetta's mothering and concern over them. She straightened the covers on their beds, tucked them in and made them a hot, quieting drink of spicy herbs.

Judy gave a contented sigh when Rosetta dragged a cot into their room and placed it in front of their window. Then Rosetta went out and returned with a machete, the knife of the tropics justly famed for its sharp, double edged blade, which she parked grimly under her bed within easy reach of her capable hand.

"I sleep here while the *Señora* is away," she announced cheerfully. "You go to sleep now. I take good care of you."

Susanne called over to Judy, "Things aren't as bad as they might be. That old thief isn't coming back to this room, for there's nothing more he wants. And even if he has the key he can't steal the idol so long as Pedro and José are guarding the monastery. Cheer up, Judy. It might be a thousand times worse."

"I suppose it could be," Judy said faintly. "I'm glad the idol is safe. Nothing else matters very much. I'm wondering if it could be Ricardo who stole the key? He might have been the thief."

"I don't want it to be that handsome Indian," Susanne said slowly. "I liked the looks of him a lot. I don't care what Pedro said, I believe he is all right."

Rosetta raised her head. "Go to sleep. Talk no more about the thief," she scolded. "You shut your eyes and go to sleep. You want old Rosetta to paddle you? She will, if you not shut your eyes."

Judy snuggled down under her covers. "All right, we'll be good. You're the grandest, nicest person that ever was, Rosetta. We like you very much. Good night, Rosetta."

"Good night, *Señoritas*," Rosetta said in her soft, warm voice. "Good night."

When Judy awoke, the sun was shining brightly and a breeze was swaying the white dotted Swiss curtains, wafting the fragrance of flowers into the room.

It was so lovely, so peaceful, for a moment it seemed as though the terror of the night must have been a dream. But the sight of Rosetta's empty cot with the machete underneath, made her realize that the horror had been all too true.

She glanced at her wrist watch and slid to the edge of the bed. "Hi, Susanne," she called. "It's eight o'clock. Phil will be down stairs waiting for us. Get up, Susanne. Hear me?"

Susanne scrambled out in a hurry. "I should say Phil will be waiting for us! By the time we have breakfast it will be late to start on that long ride to the second river. We'll have to get a wiggle on."

They found Phil perched on the stone balustrade of the corridor. "Hi, you lazy things!" he called, getting off and walking down to meet them. "My gosh, I thought you were going to sleep all day. Did you forget you had a date with important me?" he asked with a broad grin.

Judy said gravely, "If you had been up almost all night, you'd be sleeping yet. A terrible thing happened. Something perfectly terrible, Phil."

"It did? I didn't—What—what happened, Judy?" Phil stammered.

Judy stared at the confused, flushed boy. "A man climbed into our room last night and stole the key to the monastery."

Phil looked horrified. "A thief was in your room!" he gasped. "He might have killed you girls! Gosh, that was a fierce thing for you to go through."

"I thought he was going to kill us," Susanne said, then went on relating the details. Phil was standing with his hands in his pockets listening, Judy, leaning against the balustrade watched the expression on Phil's face.

What had he started to say? she wondered. Why had he been so confused? Phil was now looking very much concerned, really horror-stricken over what Susanne was telling.

He turned to Judy, "You shouldn't have taken charge of the key. That was a fool thing for you to do."

"It wasn't a fool thing," she flared. "And not a thing would have happened if I hadn't been careless enough to talk about it. I don't need advice from anyone, thank you."

"I know you don't," Phil said slowly. "I said that because I don't want anything to happen to you girls. Something almost did."

There was concern on his face. But something else was worrying Phil. He kept glancing around and seemed uneasy. Judy was puzzled.

Susanne told him, "You'll be sorry on your own account, Phil, that the key was stolen, for we were planning to stop at the monastery and show you the idol."

Phil looked surprised and tremendously pleased. "You were?" he said. "That would have been swell of you. Thanks just the same. And I want to tell you what bricks you girls are. Not many would be going for a ride if they had had the experience you had last night. Almost any other girl would be sick in bed."

Judy gave him a sharp look. "I'm going to have my breakfast," she said abruptly and went down the steps into the bright sunlight of the patio.

Phil's eyes followed the khaki-clad little figure walking down the flower-lined path. "Whew, she's jittery after all." Then he said that they had better hurry with their breakfast for if they didn't start soon they would have to shorten their ride. He could hardly wait to show them that trail as it was one of the most beautiful in this section.

"We can hardly wait either," Susanne told him as they hurried down the steps. "Ever since we came we've wanted to take that ride, but Uncle Jim said it was too far for us to go alone."

Marie, who was setting the table was on her way back to the kitchen. Judy saw her stop and look intently at a large rose bush growing in front of the balustrade. Judy's keen eyes also caught a glimpse of something blue among the green leaves. With a cry, she skirted the fountain and ran over to the place, but Marie was there before her. The Indian girl thrust her hand between the branches and pulled out Judy's blue slipper.

"Oh Marie, it's mine," Judy cried joyously. "Susanne, Phil, here's my slipper. The key must be near here too. Come quick and help hunt!"

As the thief probably had dropped the slipper when he slid down the post, they felt certain that the key was caught in some nearby bush, or had dropped between the branches to the ground.

"He stole both your slippers," Susanne said. "He may still have the one with the key in it."

Judy's heart sank. "That's right; he may not have dropped the one we want, but there is a chance."

In spite of the thorns, they ran their hands inside separating the branches so they might see between. They felt underneath, searching feverishly, not only there, but among the yellow and white honeysuckle vines and flowerbeds.

Susanne's grimy fingers were going over the grass near a flaming hibiscus shrub. "Please move, Marie. The key may have landed way over here."

Marie's slender, bare feet moved very slowly, then like a flash, she stooped down and picked up something.

"Here is the key," she said in her low, throaty

voice. "Señorita, I thought I was standing on a little stone."

For a few minutes bedlam broke loose. Phil had his arms around Judy. Susanne was holding the key high showing it to Rosetta who was running across the courtyard.

They were too overjoyed, too excited to eat much breakfast. They were eager to ride to the monastery and tell the good news to José.

"Where's Pedro?" Judy asked Rosetta, slipping a corner of her green handkerchief through the handle of the little brass key, then tying the key fast with a hard knot.

"Pedro has not come home, Señorita," Rosetta told her. "But do not worry, if he is not at the monastery, he will not be far away."

"If he comes, don't tell him we found the key, Rosetta. We want the fun of telling him ourselves," Judy said. She stuck the key and handkerchief into the breast pocket of her shirt and buttoned the flap. "There, it is safe now. It can't possibly get out of this place."

"You and Phil go along to the corral, I'll catch up with you," Susanne told them. "I'm after my kodak. If it's light enough we'll take pictures of the idol."

Phil called as she ran across the courtyard,

"You're a bright kid for thinking of that. You have brains under that blond thatch of yours."

"Sure!" Susanne yelled back. "Are you just finding that out?"

"That was a swell thought of Susanne," Judy said. "The pictures will be something to show when we get home and they'll be a lovely gift for Colonel Thompson."

Judy was so excited, so happy, that not until they were riding down the trail did Phil's peculiar actions bother her again. Why had he stammered so when Suzanne told him about the theft? What had he started to say? 'I didn't—I didn't—' what? Why had he been so confused? He had shown sympathy, but also he had shown uneasiness. There was something strange about this, something she could not understand. She drew a sharp breath and glanced at the brown eyed, handsome boy astride the dapple gray horse. He was laughing and talking to Susanne, apparently happy and carefree. Just the same his actions still troubled her and she was sorry they were going to show him the idol.

"Look out for that low limb!" Susanne called, when they turned on the little path which led to the entrance of the monastery. "Ugh, these wet vines feel like snakes when they slap against my face. Isn't this the dampiest, spookiest, smelliest old building that ever was? I hate it."

They found José almost asleep, squatting beside the door of the strong room.

Judy was furious. "Isn't he the limit!" she stormed. "Look at him sitting there with his eyes shut. I don't call him much of a guard."

Only José's little black eyes showed any emotion when they told him the great news.

"I go home now," he said, picking up his machete.

Judy waved her riding crop impatiently, "Yes, yes, go on. We shan't need you any longer. If you see Pedro don't tell him we found the key. Do you understand?"

"Si, si. I understand, Señorita. I not tell."

"Very well. Trot along now, José."

Phil held out his hand for the key. "I'll open the door, Judy."

Susanne was examining the lock. "There's one thing certain, this lock hasn't been tampered with. I'll bet dear old Pedro scared the thief so he's running yet."

"I hope he is," Judy said, as she watched Phil put the key in the lock and turn it. "I don't want him anywhere around this plantation. That old fellow scared me enough."

Phil pulled the door open. He insisted upon

going in first. "There isn't anything to be scared of," he said with a grin, "except mice. I'll go ahead and frighten them away."

"For heaven's sake, are there mice in there!" Susanne peered through the open doorway.

Judy gave her a push. "Don't stand there. Go on in, Susanne. What if there are mice, they can't hurt you."

When they entered the chapel and saw that the leather bag was still in the corner where it had been placed by Colonel Thompson, Judy was so happy, so relieved she ran over and patted it.

"I really didn't doubt you were here, but oh it's wonderful to see you again, you nice old saddle-bag. All right, Phil, take it. Be careful when you set it on the table. We don't want to break the idol."

"I'll be careful," Phil told her as he carried it over to the refectory table. "It's heavy, isn't it? Gosh, I can hardly wait to see this old War God. Here, let me undo those straps. Judy, you're so excited your fingers are all thumbs."

Judy laughed. "I'm excited all right. I'll be so glad to see the idol again, I'll probably hug it."

"I shan't," Susanne said. "I don't want to get any nearer to that terrible old thing than I have to."

Judy lifted out the cloth covered idol and held

it while Phil unwound the long strip of cotton. When he finished, Judy held it up for his inspection. "Phil Stanton, did you ever see anything so gorgeous! Look at the jewels. See them?"

Phil was gazing at it with fascinated eyes. "Oh boy, it's a corker! I've seen heaps of them, but in all my life, I've never seen one all dripping with jewels."

Susanne backed away. "You've seen it now, so let's take the pictures and get out of here. I don't like that old War God." She walked across the room to where a shaft of sunlight was streaming in through a window. "If you bring it over here, Phil, I think I'll be able to get some good pictures."

She took one of Phil holding the idol, then of Judy holding it in her hands. They could not induce Susanne to have her picture taken with it, and as soon as they had finished, she said. "Let's not fool around in here. Put that old idol back into the saddlebag and let's get out. I'm scared to death of that fierce looking thing. I wouldn't touch it for a million dollars!"

Judy laughed at her. "Well Susanne, you're missing something. His body is so smooth I love to touch it. Phil you rub your hands down his back and feel how slick and smooth it is."

Phil ran his fingers over the idol's highly polished back. "It sure is slick. It's as slippery as a chunk of ice. I like the feel of it too, Judy."

Judy leaned down and looked hard into the shining, yellow eyes of the jade idol. "Hey, you! I'm not afraid of you, even though you are glaring at me as though you'd like to kill me. You're nothing but a piece of jade. And those yellow eyes of yours aren't real either. They're only amber. So—"

"So nuts to you, old chap!" Phil broke in laughing. "That's what I say too, Judy. He's like one of the 'profs' at our military academy. He looks fierce, and is just a big bluff." He lifted the long strip of cloth from the table. "Come on, Judy, we'll wrap him up again, so Susanne can't see him. She's so scared of him we'll be good to her."

Judy sighed. "I'm sorry to leave so soon. We'll never have another chance to see such a gorgeous thing as this." She took the cloth from Phil and started to wrap up the War God.

Susanne was standing with her back to them pretending to be much interested in one of the windows. Judy laughed at her. "His head's covered, Susanne. We can't see his yellow eyes. . . . I'm now winding the cloth around his green body. . . . You'll be glad to know that the snakes are almost hidden. . . . Now, he's completely and neatly wrapped up. He looks like a nice little mummy, doesn't he, Phil?"

"He sure does," Phil said, placing the idol very carefully in the saddlebag. "Now I'll carry His Majesty over to his hiding place in the corner."

Something very strange happened a few minutes later. They were untying their horses when Phil said, "I must go home for a little while. Will you mind if I don't go riding this morning?"

Susanne looked at him anxiously, "Are you sick, Phil? Aren't you feeling well?"

"Sure, sure, I'm okay." Phil was eyeing them to see how they were taking it. "Sorry as the dickens to disappoint you. But I have to go home for something. I mean after something— to attend to something," he blundered on. "I'll be back right after lunch, or a little later. This afternoon we'll play tennis, go swimming, or do anything else you like. Do you mind very much?"

"Of course not," Susanne told him. "I'm glad you aren't sick. You had me worried for a minute."

Judy mounted her horse. "I don't care what you do," she said with a shrug of her shoulders as she started King on a gallop out of the courtyard.

Susanne put her foot in the stirrup and swung up on her saddle. "Poor old Judy's still jittery, isn't she?" She smiled down at Phil. "It's perfectly all right to postpone our ride until tomorrow. We'll be looking for you this afternoon, Phil. We'll go swimming again. Good-bye until then."

Judy was home ahead of her. Susanne found her sitting at the breakfast table having more coffee and toast.

Judy jabbed a spoon viciously into the marmalade jar and stormed at Susanne. "If you aren't the softy, Susanne Lawrence! You're about the easiest thing I know.

Susanne's blue eyes tore open. "What have I done? What's the matter now?"

"Being so nice to Phil after the way he's acted."

Susanne's face was blank. "I haven't seen anything wrong about Phil."

Judy leaned across the table. "Didn't you hear him stammer 'I didn't—' when you told him something terrible had happened? What did he mean by that? Why didn't he go on and finish what he started to say? Why did he get so red in the face and act so confused? Yes, and what made him change his mind just now and not go on our ride? Why didn't he tell the reason he had to go home?"

"I'm sure I don't know. But I don't see why you're talking about such a little thing. And as far as saying 'I didn't,' and then stopping, that doesn't mean anything either. Your imagination is working overtime this morning, Judy."

"It isn't," Judy said. "And listen to this—"

She stopped talking, for Marie had come from the kitchen with a pot of hot coffee.

Her dark eyes were full of excitement and her pretty face was flushed, "I have something to tell you," she announced breathlessly, as she carefully set the silver pot down on the table. "Señoritas, you must never, never touch the War God! If you as much as put one finger on it, terrible things will happen to you."

Susanne looked up startled. "Not touch the War God? Who told you such an idiotic thing?"

"It is written under one of the hearts hanging on his necklace. It is so, Señorita."

Judy put a lump of sugar into her coffee and said calmly, "Well, we don't believe you, Marie. In the first place I don't think any thing like that is under one of the hearts. That's only more of your silly gossip. You're all so superstitious. Always talking about the evil eye and other such tommyrot. Don't go spreading such a crazy thing around."

Susanne laughed. "For pity's sake, don't stop her, Judy! If every one believes that, they won't try to steal the idol." She motioned with her hand. "Tell it, Marie. Start out right now and spread the good news."

Marie did not laugh. She stood there twisting the corner of her white apron and saying earnestly, "It is true, Señoritas. It is written under one of the hearts. I beg of you not to touch it. Here is Pedro. He will tell you so too. Pedro," she called, "come here, please."

Pedro came down the path, his wrinkled face all smiles. "Very happy I am, Señoritas. José told me you found the key."

"Yes, we found it, Pedro. It was over by that hibiscus bush. Marie is telling us the craziest thing. Go on, Marie, tell him what you just said to us."

"I said to them that they must not touch the War God."

Pedro nodded his head. "Si, si, Marie is telling you what is true. But you will not touch it, Señorita. Pedro is not worried about that."

Judy drew a long breath. "I touched it, Pedro. I held it in my hands. I—I am not afraid. There is nothing to such superstition."

Pedro's black eyes widened in horror.

"Señorita, you touched it! You touched it! Madre de Dios!" Throwing up his hands and calling on all the saints to preserve her, Pedro ran from the courtyard.

CHAPTER IV

AN EMPTY SADDLEBAG

Judy's lips were twitching, but she was smiling at Susanne and saying, "There's nothing to it. It's only superstition, isn't it? I'm—I'm not afraid. I know that—"

Abruptly, she shoved back her chair and started for the house. Susanne rushed after her.

"Judy dear, you mustn't believe all that silly stuff. You said yourself it was only superstition. There's nothing to it at all. You know that, don't you?"

Tears filled Judy's eyes. "Yes, I know it, Susanne. It's upsetting me because I'm so worn out and nervous. I want to go home." She rubbed a hand across both wet cheeks. "I want to go home, Susanne."

Susanne's arm went around her. "Of course you do. I'd like to go, too. But we can't leave right away, can we? You come into the living room and lie down. You need a good, long sleep. I shouldn't have made you get up this morning. After what you went through last night, that was

62

a thoughtless thing for me to do. You'll feel better when you've had a rest and sleep."

The living room, with its gay chintz draperies, its books, its low, easy chairs and vases of pink roses and tall, golden lilies, was a charming, homey place.

Rosetta came hurrying in. Her face full of compassion and anxiety for Judy. "We take you upstairs and put you to bed," she said, her arm around the now sobbing girl.

Susanne shook her head. She was keeping Judy away from the room in which she had had the terrifying experience. "It is cooler down here, Rosetta. Judy will be more comfortable here in the sitting room. I'll run up and get her pajamas, while you undress her."

When Judy was lying on the broad, linen covered sofa, Susanne pulled down the Venetian blinds to shut out the light, then tiptoed over and kissed the hot, tear stained face.

"I never was such a baby before. But I'm tired. So tired, Susanne, and nervous. I never was—so tired."

This was a new Judy to Susanne. Judy had always been strong, sure of herself. Nothing had ever bothered Judy. For the first time in her life, Susanne was now seeing Judy afraid. Judy, who laughed at fear, was now lying here shaken and terror-stricken.

"Of course, you're exhausted, honey. I'm leaving you now. It's cool and dark in here, just right for a nice long sleep."

Rosetta had disappeared, but Marie was clearing away the breakfast things, when Susanne went out of the living room. She started across the courtyard to question her further, then turned back. What good would it do? Marie would only say the same thing over again.

So much had happened, Susanne was feeling nervous and restless, and a little afraid. It wasn't only idle gossip, that a warning was written under one of the hearts. Pedro wouldn't say so, if it were not true.

She went up to their room and changed into a cool, light blue voile. On the corridor again, she wandered around restlessly for a few minutes, then busied herself with refilling the vases and bowls with flowers. Out in the patio she cut flaming red camellias, pansies, pink and white roses, larkspur and purple and gold iris. There had to be many flowers scattered everywhere, to make the house gay and cheery.

She wondered what Phil was doing. It was only 10:30, and she could hardly wait for him to return. If only he would explain why he had to go home, it would make Judy feel so much better. Poor Phil didn't dream Judy was suspicious of him. If he did, he would explain everything eagerly, to get that out of her mind.

Judy was still sound asleep when Susanne had finished with the flowers. She tiptoed out of the room after carrying in the refilled vases, happy that Judy was getting her much needed rest.

It occurred to Susanne what she could do now to pass away the time. She would develop her films and print some of the pictures. Removing the roll of films from her camera, she went up to a large closet which her aunt had allowed them to turn into a dark room.

While she was developing and printing the pictures, she tried to figure out who the thief might be. She wondered too, why Phil hadn't told them his reason for going home, but most of all, her mind was on Marie's warning.

She had not touched the idol, so was not afraid for herself. But Judy and Phil, Uncle Jim and Colonel Thompson, had held it. What horrible thing was going to happen to them? She said to herself fiercely, "That War God is only a piece of jade. It hasn't the power to hurt anyone of them. I know it hasn't."

She found she had five excellent views of the idol. Two, with Phil holding it, one with Judy and two of the idol alone. There was a picture of Judy, laughing, carefree and happy, riding up the trail on King. And there was old Pedro, squinting and wrinkling up his face, as he always did when he looked at you.

When Susanne went to the living room, to her joy, she found an awake, cheerful girl. A Judy who was not longing to go home, and who laughed at the idea that harm could come to them on account of the idol.

"I'm ashamed of the way I acted, Susanne," she said, sitting up on the couch. "I'm not weak minded enough to believe in such silly superstition."

Susanne pulled up the Venetian blinds, and a shaft of sunlight came into the room. "Of course you're not weak minded enough to believe such trash. And darling, from now on, you're going to have a grand day. I've a surprise to show you after lunch. And this afternoon when Phil comes, we're going for a grand old swim."

The usually happy Marie was very sober as she waited on the table. It made Susanne nervous, the pathetic way in which the Indian girl looked at Judy. But Judy was in high spirits and did not seem to notice Marie's change of manner.

Judy was delighted with the pictures, and after lunch she and Susanne printed more until it was almost time for Phil to come. Judy brought out her bathing suit and threw it across a chair.

"If ever Phil wants to make it right with me, he'll have to explain why he ran off the way he did this morning," she stormed. "I'm happy until I think of him, then I become perfectly furious."

Susanne pulled off a blue and yellow sock. "Oh calm down. What do you care whether he explains or not. Someone's knocking. Come in!" she called.

It was Rosetta. "Tomoso wants the key to the strong room. He is down in the courtyard waiting, Señorita," she said to Judy.

Judy asked, "Who on earth is Tomoso? And why is he asking for the key, Rosetta? I'm not giving the key to anyone but Colonel Thompson and Uncle Jim."

A surprised look came on Rosetta's bland face. "You not know Tomoso? He is Colonel Thompson's mozo. He has worked for the Señor many years. The Señor wants to show the idol to a friend, so Tomoso has come after the key. In a hurry he is, Señorita."

"You're sure Tomoso is telling the truth?"

"Tomoso is a good Indian. He would not do anything wrong."

Judy took the key from her pajama pocket, unknotted the corner of the handkerchief and handed the key to Rosetta. "I don't like to do this. I'm hoping it's all right."

Rosetta waddled out of the room. "It is all right, Señorita," she said in a grieved voice. "When Rosetta says a thing is so, it is so."

An idea suddenly came to Susanne. "Let's go to the monastery and give Colonel Thompson the pictures. What do you say?" she asked eagerly.

"Fine!" Judy ran to the window and saw an Indian as old as Pedro mounting a large, gray mule. "Tomoso! Are you Tomoso?" she called.

The old fellow's beady eyes looked up at her. "Si, Señorita. I am Tomoso."

"All right. You tell Colonel Thompson that we're coming too. We have a present for him. Understand?"

"Si. I tell him, Señorita."

Instead of her jodhpurs, it was a pair of white slacks Judy saw first when she opened the closet door. So it was slacks she got into. She slipped on a green sweater, combed her wavy, long bob, and tied a green ribbon around her head. As usual, she looked like a gay, pretty gypsy. Susanne, in her breeches, riding boots and white shirt, resembled a lovely little patrician.

Riding down the trail Susanne asked, "Judy, do you suppose the Colonel has heard about the thief getting into our room? If he has, you'll never get that key again   He'll be too afraid something might happen to you."

Judy's heart sank. "I'll bet he has. I'll feel terrible if I have to give up the key. I want to have charge of the idol until he takes it to Mexico City. When I start a thing I want to go through with it. Oh, let's hope he hasn't, Susanne. Let's hope he hasn't heard."

The vision of Rosetta guarding their bedroom window with her fierce looking knife came to Susanne and she laughed. "You tell Colonel Thompson about our bodyguard, and he'll let you keep the key. He'll know we'll be safe from now on."

Susanne was wondering whether Colonel Thompson had seen the warning written under one of the hearts hanging on the idol. He hadn't seemed afraid to touch it, so evidently, if he had seen it it wasn't troubling him.

She thought of King Tut, of the curse written on the door of the tomb. Hadn't she read somewhere that every man who helped uncover that tomb had died an unusual death? She tried to recall exactly what she had read. She was not certain, but she knew that something tragic had happened to every man. That might have been only newspaper talk. Or, what ever happened, might have occurred anyway. Her common sense told her that a curse could not harm anyone. It was all superstitious nonsense. But just the same, it did not make her feel very easy.

Judy called, "Hi, Susanne, in our excitement, we forgot all about Phil. Hope he comes soon and has to sit there cooling his heels. After we've seen Colonel Thompson let's go for a ride without old Phil. It would be just what he deserves."

"You old mean thing you," Susanne laughed. "I wouldn't do that for anything. We're going to hustle back to the house soon as we give Colonel Thompson these pictures."

When they rode into the courtyard of the monastery they found Colonel Thompson and a slender, scholarly looking man standing in the cloister waiting for them.

Judy called gaily, "Good morning, Colonel."

"Good morning. Hope you're glad to see us," Susanne said, smiling at him. "You better be, for we've a wonderful present for you. It's something we know you'll like."

The men came down the steps of the cloister and walked over to them.

"Good morning, girls. I'm mighty glad you're here." Colonel Thompson's voice showed his relief. "Tom, here are the guardians of the idol, Miss Judy Winslow and Miss Susanne Lawrence. Girls, this is Mr. Garwood." He pulled a handkerchief from his pocket and mopped his shiny, bald head. "That was a stiff joke you played on us, young ladies. Even though you are grown up, you deserve to be spanked."

The girls were leaning down shaking hands with the smiling guest.

"I don't call that a polite way to talk, do you, Mr. Garwood?" Judy said. "We haven't played any joke. What does he mean?"

The Colonel's right hand was nervously patting Judy's saddle. "Please, please, I beg you not to keep this up any longer. I must hurry back to my work."

Judy looked at him puzzled. "I don't know what you mean, Colonel Thompson."

"You know well enough what I mean," the Colonel's voice was impatient. "We know you have brought the idol, but sending a key to an empty room was rather a poor joke. I don't think much of—"

Judy gripped his hand. "An empty room? We haven't the idol! What do you mean?"

The Colonel's voice trembled. "Your message—What have you brought?"

"What have we brought? Oh Colonel Thompson, only pictures, that's all!"

She slid off her horse and went racing across the courtyard to the cloister. "I know it's there!

Come with me, I'll show you where it is. It couldn't have disappeared, for we saw it only a few hours ago."

Susanne, the Colonel and Mr. Garwood were in the chapel almost as soon as Judy.

In the corner was the saddlebag, limp, empty.

Judy ran over and felt inside, even though it was perfectly obvious the idol was not in there.

"It couldn't get away. It couldn't get out of here. Truly, Colonel Thompson, we saw it only a few hours ago. It was right in this saddlebag."

"Well it isn't there now." The Colonel's voice was sharp. "No use in having hysterics, Judy. We must keep calm and try to figure out how the thief got in here."

Mr. Garwood asked gently, "I am wondering if you happened to loan the key today for a few minutes."

Susanne looked at him horrified. "Of course not. We wouldn't do such a thing. Judy had the key the whole time, except—" She looked helplessly at Judy. They had intended to keep this quiet and now she had to tell. She went on reluctantly, "A man got into our room last night and stole the key. But this morning we—"

"A man got into your room last night?" he asked in alarm.

Susanne went on quickly, "Yes, but he stole only the key.   He didn't hurt us."

"He might have killed you.   I hadn't any right to place you in such grave danger.   Did you hide the key in your blue slipper?"

Judy nodded.   "Yes, that's where I put it."

"How on earth did anyone know you had it and know where it was?"

"He must have heard us talking.   We were fooling about it up in our room."

"Fooling about such an important thing!" The Colonel was looking at her in astonishment. "I thought you had better sense than that.   Who was upstairs, and how did you happen to have the key this morning?"

Judy told him that Phil Stanton was home and that he was with them yesterday.   He was upstairs getting into their Uncle Jim's bathing trunks when the girls were talking about the key, and was also present when they found the slipper and key in the patio where the thief had dropped them.

Susanne burst out, "I just thought of something.   Do you suppose Phil locked the door of the strong room this morning?   If he didn't that's how—"

"The strong room?   Do you mean to say that

you brought Phil down here?" Colonel Thompson asked.

"Yes. Do you mind?" Judy was conscience stricken. "He told us that Uncle Jim always showed him the treasures that were in here, so we thought it was all right."

"He did a strange thing, Colonel Thompson." Susanne had not meant to say that. It had slipped out. She gave Judy a quick, startled glance. "It wasn't anything. It really isn't worth telling," she added quickly.

Colonel Thompson had seen the glance. He asked quietly, "Go on, Susanne. What happened after you showed him the idol?"

"Nothing—much," Susanne said uneasily.

"What happened?" the Colonel insisted. "I must know, Susanne."

Susanne went on slowly, "We were going for a ride to the second river, but after showing him the idol he said we would have to postpone it, that he was going home."

"Why?"

Susanne looked at him pleadingly. "I don't know. He didn't explain. I'm sorry you're making me say this. I don't believe Phil would do anything wrong. Truly, I don't."

The Colonel said gravely, "I'd feel sorry to think he would. But look." He pointed to the windows. "Do you see those stone bars and that the vines haven't been disturbed? The thief did not get into the chapel that way, or by the barred door. One can't come by any other conclusion but that he entered this room the same way we did. Judy had the key. So I am convinced Phil did not lock the door. It may have been unintentional, very likely it was. But I—"

Susanne was almost in tears. "I'm sure he meant to lock it," she said. "It does look queer he didn't tell why he had to go home. But he'll explain when he comes back. I know he will." She was glad she hadn't told of Judy's suspicions of him that morning.

To her dismay, Judy was telling it now. An angry, suspicious Judy. She ended her story by saying, "I know it wasn't Phil who stole the key, for the man was much taller. But I'm sure Phil had something to do with it."

Susanne's face brightened, "The door was locked when you arrived, Colonel Thompson, so Phil did lock it after all." She was happy she had thought of this."

"It has a spring lock," the Colonel told her. "All one has to do is to snap it shut. It may be he left the door unlocked unintentionally and one of the Indians stole the idol. I'm going up to where they're picking coffee and offer a reward, of $500 for the return of the idol and $200 for the capture of the thief. You girls go back to the house. No doubt you'll find Phil there. Now this is most important. I don't want you to mention the idol to Phil. I don't want him to know that you have heard that the idol has been stolen. Another thing, be sure to keep him at the house until we come."

CHAPTER V

A REWARD IS OFFERED

THEY RODE back to the house crushed over the disappearance of the idol, and sick with remorse over failing in their responsibility.

For a time there was silence, then Judy said in a broken voice, "I wish I were dead, Susanne."

Susanne scolded, "Don't talk so silly. Don't you ever, ever say such a thing again. But Judy, we just mustn't think Phil had anything to do with this. We just mustn't."

Judy too had been thinking of Phil. From the first, she had liked him very much. Now her mind was filled with questions. Why had he acted so strangely when she told him that something terrible had happened? And why had he changed his mind about going riding after he had seen the idol? Why hadn't he told the reason he had to go home? "I don't know what to think," she said to Susanne. I don't want him to be the thief anymore than you do, Susanne. I'm sure he'll keep his word and be at the house waiting for us. And if he doesn't explain before, he'll straighten everything out when Colonel

Thompson questions him. Let's not worry."

Susanne glanced at her wrist watch. "My glory, it's after three o'clock. Phil's had a good long wait, hasn't he?"

Judy was so eager to learn if Phil really had arrived she passed Susanne and was the first to gallop into the courtyard.

But there was no iron-gray horse, there was no Phil. Judy was not only sick with disappointment, but furious.

Susanne came through the archway in a cloud of dust. "Hi, is he here?" she called.

Judy turned, her eyes flashing. "Can't you see he isn't? Now, what do you think?"

"He might have been here and gone," Susanne said weakly.

"If he had he would have left a note. He wouldn't even have done that," she corrected herself. "He would have waited right here for us. You see, he didn't keep his word. He had no intention of coming back. He's away hiding his precious loot. That's where he is." She clapped her hands three times for someone to come and take their horses. "Where under heaven's name are Pedro and José! Not even Rosetta is around, nor the cook, nor Marie."

Susanne was stunned. She had been so sure Phil would be here.

"How would I know where the servants are," she said slowly. "You get off and I'll take the horses around to the back patio. Judy, I want to tell you something. I can't believe Phil would steal. Give him a chance to explain before you condemn him. Don't be unfair, Judy."

Judy slid off King. "You make me sick," she said angrily. "You believe in him because he has nice manners and is good looking. Why didn't he tell the reason he had to go home? Why didn't he keep his word and come back in the afternoon?"

Susanne sighed as she reached up and took hold of King's bridle. "For heaven's sake, don't ask me those questions. You know I can't answer them. But just the same I want you to be a good sport and give him a chance to explain. He will, Judy. He'll tell us why he—"

Judy broke in. "Here's another thing. How could anyone else get into the chapel? He left the door unlocked, then went back and stole the idol. For the love of Mike, stop standing up for him!" Suddenly, it occurred to her how she could find out where he was. "Oh Susanne, I just thought of something. I'm going to telephone their plantation. You throw the reins across the rosebush. The horses will stand all right."

Eager to get in touch with Phil, they raced into

the living room and breathlessly, Judy lifted the receiver. "Hello. . . . Hello. . . . Mr. Stanton's plantation, please." In a few minutes, she was asking, "Is this Mr. Stanton? This is Judy Winslow, Mr. Harrington's niece. . . . Oh yes, thank you, we're having a very nice time. . . . Yes indeed, we love Mexico. . . . We are staying all summer. . . . Yes, until school begins. . . . I'm calling up about Phil. He was here this morning and said he would return this afternoon to play tennis with my cousin and me. He hasn't come. Do you know what his plans are? . . . Oh, he has!" she exclaimed in a startled voice. "All by himself! . . . Don't you know where? . . . He didn't tell you? . . . When do you expect him back? . . . All right. Thank you, Mr. Stanton."

She hung up the receiver and turned to Susanne. "My word, if that isn't something!" she gasped.

Susanne slid off the arm of a chintz covered chair and grabbed Judy. "What did he say? For heaven's sake tell me."

Judy answered soberly, "Phil's taken a canoe and gone up El Tigre river. He didn't tell his father where he was bound for, nor when he would be back. He said he might be gone for several days. Oh Susanne, now I know he has the idol and has taken it up there to hide it."

Susanne stared at Judy. It would be terrible if it were true. However she was not thinking of that now, but something vastly more important. "He shouldn't have gone up there, Judy. Don't you remember what Uncle Jim told us about El Tigre? He told us that it isn't safe for any white person to go up into that wild region. And Phil's all alone. He has a peach of a father! He isn't worried one bit, is he! I'll bet if Phil's mother were living he wouldn't have gone off by himself."

Judy dropped onto a chair and glared at her. "You would talk like that! You would! You're a silly thing to waste your sympathy on such a fellow as Phil Stanton. He knows where he's going all right. If it's that dangerous, with all the Indians they have on their place he'd have taken one quickly enough, if he weren't doing something he wanted to keep secret. Susanne, if ever I lay eyes on him again he'll hear what I think of him! I know why he went up that river alone, and so do you. No Indian stole that idol."

Susanne walked over to the doorway and was looking out into the sunlit patio. "All right, Judy, have it your own way," she said slowly. "Phil did it. Now, I hope that makes you feel better."

"It doesn't. It makes me feel worse," Judy said miserably. "It would be bad enough to have a stranger steal it, but a boy you've been swimming with, and trusted so much, you showed him the idol. It makes you darned sick!"

She wondered whether they could discover the place where Phil had taken the idol. If only they could find it. Her thoughts flew to the reward. If she were mistaken and an Indian did steal it, the money Colonel Thompson was offering might prove tempting enough to get it back. Suddenly, it occurred to her something she could do to help. She had money of her own. Excitedly, she sprang to her feet.

"Susanne, I'm going to add $50.00 to the reward Colonel Thompson is giving! I have that much to do with as I please. If we take the short cut we can get to the weighing place before he does." Tears welled in her eyes. "I'm sorry I haven't a million dollars to offer. Oh Susanne, I can't tell you how terribly I feel. I—"

Susanne's arm went around her. "Of course you do. I feel badly too, Judy. But we were not to blame." Trying to make her voice sound more assuring than she felt, she went on, "And don't you worry, that reward will get back the idol. I'm sure of it, honey." She glanced down at the ring on the little finger of her left hand; it was a square cut diamond flanked by two emeralds. Could she part with it? Could she bring herself to give it up? It was the most costly thing she owned. Not only the most expensive, but the thing she cared for most. Her parents had given it to her on her last birthday. She knew them well enough to realize that under the circumstances, they would understand and not scold. Slowly, she pulled it off. "I want you to take this and offer it too," she said in almost a whisper.

Judy put her hands behind her back. "Oh no, not your ring, Susanne. I'll not take it. Don't be foolish. I know how much you think of it, so don't try to make me take your ring."

Susanne slipped the ring into Judy's shirt pocket. "You are taking it. And we won't argue over this any longer. I'm as responsible as you are. So, you keep that ring, or I'll never speak to you again as long as I live!"

Judy grabbed Susanne by the shoulders and kissed her pretty flushed face. "You're a crazy little nut, to give this away, and I ought to be killed for taking it. But I shall, Susanne. I know how you feel. Bless your generous old heart. Come on, we must beat it now if we want to get there at the same time as Colonel Thompson."

As they had hoped, they met the Colonel and Mr. Garwood before the two men had arrived at the weighing place. They told them about Phil and that they wanted to add to the reward.

When Susanne offered her ring and Judy told of her $50.00, Colonel Thompson protested, but the girls were so insistent, that he finally gave in.

In a few minutes they were riding into a clearing where Indians were carrying filled burlap bags to a long table. At one end, a flashing eyed mozo was busy with the scales, while at the other, Carlos, the superintendent, sat in state under an enormous yellow umbrella. He was checking the pickers and marking the number of pounds of coffee in each bag.

Surprised and pleased to see his visitors, Carlos rose to his feet and stood there smiling. But it was a different Carlos who called his workers together a few minutes later. His swarthy face was livid with fury as he sprang up on the table and jerked a whistle from his pocket.

There was no doubt in his mind but what one of the coffee pickers had taken the idol and his threats were so dire and terrifying, shivers went up and down Judy's spine.

She sat astride King watching the men, women and children as they came running down between the red berry covered trees.

Nearly two hundred had arrived before she

saw anyone she knew. Then Marie and Ricardo appeared, not hurrying at all, but walking hand in hand and making a great show of laughing and talking. They stood in the rear from where Marie smiled at her, but Ricardo never looked in her direction. Pedro came soon after. He was too old to run so fast and was panting hard.

Carlos spoke rapidly and loudly. Only because Colonel Thompson insisted, did he tell of the reward and hold up the diamond ring for their inspection. He said if the thief did not return the idol he would keep after him until he was run down, and when caught the scoundrel's hands would be cut off. If the idol were returned at once, the Señor would give the thief this reward, and, although the fellow did not deserve it, he would go unpunished.

He dismissed them with a wave of his hands. "Vamos now, and remember what I told you!" he shouted.

Riding back to the house Susanne said she was weak all over. She had never heard such terrifying threats.

"He certainly didn't mince matters," the Colonel said. "The threat to cut off the thief's hands was bad enough, but the others made even my blood run cold. But that's the only way to handle these Indians. Carlos believes the same as I, that one of the coffee pickers is the guilty person. I'll wager this will bring results."

The men did not stop at the house. The Colonel told the girls that he would come by in the morning. "I want Rosetta to sleep in your room tonight and Pedro on the veranda. I'm hoping Phil will be here when I return in the morning. When he arrives don't show in any way that you are the least suspicious of him. Promise?" he asked gravely.

"We'll try," Judy told him, wondering if she could keep from showing it if Phil didn't explain right off why he went up river. "Susanne and I will try very hard."

That night it was again full moon and the patio once more was a place of loveliness. But no dark-eyed Mexican danced to soft music . . . the place lay desolate and lonely.

The girls were in the living room waiting for their aunt to call them on the telephone; Susanne wrote letters at the desk, Judy stood in the doorway looking out on the patio. She could not see Rosetta and Pedro, but could hear their voices and knew they were sitting on a bench in front of the kitchen. Their nearness gave her a sense of security.

Susanne folded her letter and slipped it into its light blue envelope, then she looked over at Judy and said, "I'm going to do something you won't like, but just the same I am going to do it. When Aunt Alice telephones I intend telling her about the key and everything that's happened. We need her desperately, Judy. I want her to come home."

Judy hurried over to her. "Oh Susanne you mustn't tell her about the key or idol! You wouldn't want Aunt Alice to leave that sick woman, would you?"

"We need her just as much as that woman," Susanne said stubbornly. "She has to come home tomorrow, Judy. I just can't stand it without her. It's perfectly terrible for us to be here all by ourselves."

Judy argued and argued. Finally, Susanne consented to keep quiet. "I guess you're right, Judy," she said to her. "It would be selfish to bring her home. I promise, I'll not tell her one thing. You don't need to worry about that, for—"

An agonizing shriek came from the back patio. Then another and still another. The girls raced to the doorway and stood there listening.

"Oh Judy, who is it, who is it?" Susanne

gasped. "Listen to her! What's happened?"

"I don't know," Judy whispered, her eyes on the entrance to the other courtyard.

The woman, now hysterical, was still shrieking and making a terrific noise. Pedro shouted at her endeavoring to calm her. Rosetta, usually so placid, was talking in a loud, excited voice.

The girls soon realized that it was old Manuela, who was doing the shrieking. When she had quieted down Pedro came trotting in to tell them what had happened.

"A ghost Manuela saw," he informed them. "A ghost, over in the dark clump of trees and bushes by the wall." He was not laughing, his wrinkled face was very serious.

Judy who was now sitting on the balustrade began to laugh. "For heaven's sake, is that what she was frightened about? She had us scared out of our wits. What was it really?"

Pedro squinted up at her. "It was a ghost, Señorita."

The smile left Susanne's face. "How do you know it was a ghost, Pedro?" she asked soberly.

"Because I saw it, Señorita." He told them that Manuela had had a good look at it when she was on her way from the kitchen to her room in the servants quarters. He, Pedro had caught only a glimpse of it before it vanished.

Believing he might have frightened the girls he said, "I did see it, Señorita. But a ghost cannot hurt anyone, so do not be afraid. Rosetta she sleep in your room tonight and old Pedro will be on the veranda, we not let anything harm you." He smiled a little. "Maybe that old ghost only want to scare Manuela. He—"

There was the tingle of the telephone. Susanne started to answer it, but Judy was there before her.

"Hello, Aunt Alice," Judy was saying in a happy voice. "We are all right. . . . You can't come home until a week from tomorrow?" Judy's voice sank. . . . "Yes, Pedro and Rosetta are taking good care of us. . . . We didn't go on our ride today. . . . Phil had to go up river. . . . Yes, we think he's swell. . . . You heard that Colonel Thompson found a jade idol and has it in the strong room? . . . Yes, we heard that too. . . . Yes, we'll try to get him to show it to us. . . . Susanne's itching to talk to you, so good-bye for now."

She gave Susanne a little poke, "Don't tell her anything to worry her," she whispered. "Please, don't tell her."

"Stop poking me. I'm not telling," Susanne whispered as she took the receiver. "Hello, Aunt Alice! . . . Yes, we're having a swell time. Judy told you all the news, so all I'm going to say is that you mustn't worry about us. Last night Rosetta brought her cot up to our room. She's sleeping in front of the window and has a machete all ready to whack any one who tries to get in. How's that for a bodyguard!" She could hear her aunt laugh.

When she hung up the receiver she turned to Judy and said with a broad grin. "Well, this little old scared-cat didn't tell, did she?"

Judy hugged her. "You were wonderful." The smile left her face. She went on soberly, "To be honest, I'm as scared as you. But we can't be selfish and take Aunt Alice away from that sick woman."

"Of course we can't," Susanne started out to the patio. "I'm going to talk to Pedro about that ghost. The moonlight's so bright it might have been nothing but a spooky shadow."

"That's right," Judy agreed. "It couldn't have been anything else."

Even though it would make the girls feel uneasy, Pedro had to be honest. "Señorita, it was not a shadow," he said. "It was a creature that had a face, a face whose eyes had been taken out."

There was very little sleep for the girls that night after such a nerve-wracking time, but the next morning, when Colonel Thompson rode into the courtyard and asked anxiously, "Are you all right? I've been worried about you." Susanne said quickly, "Oh we're just great, thank you." They were not telling about the ghost for he had enough to worry him.

"The idol has been stolen, so it doesn't make sense that anyone would bother you again," he said smiling down at them. "But in my present frame of mind I'm not capable of thinking clearly. What about Phil? Any word from him this morning?"

Judy's face flushed with anger. "No, he hasn't shown up. He's a swell person, he is!"

"Not very swell," the Colonel remarked gravely. "Want to come with me to the monastery? I want to look around there a bit."

They were eager to go. And soon they were riding down the trail talking of the reward they had offered. The Colonel was not greatly disturbed over the fact that the idol had not been returned. He felt it would take time for the thief to muster up sufficient courage to claim the reward.

Judy was thinking it will be Phil who will return the idol. He'll say he came across the place where the thief had hid it, or he'll have some other flimsy excuse for having it in his possession. Susanne also was thinking. But she was still firm in

her belief in Phil Stanton. Phil had left the door
unlocked, but it was unintentional. The thief
was an Indian, the same one who stole the key.

As always, the old chapel was dim and cool.
Although the Colonel and the girls had searched
there before, they looked again behind the baptistry and the altar and underneath the refectory
table.

Susanne was looking at one of the windows.
The bars seemed further apart in this one than
the others. She spoke of it to the Colonel and
Judy. "Don't you believe a man could squeeze
in between those bars?" she asked. "I do. I'm
sure men have escaped from prison through
smaller spaces than those up there."

Judy agreed, but said, "No one got in the
chapel that way, Susanne. Can't you see the
vines haven't been disturbed?"

Colonel Thompson was regarding the window
with interest. "By Jove, those bars are farther
apart than the others. The thief could have
pushed the vines aside, not torn them at all. I
wonder if that is the way he did—"

A shot rang out, followed by the scream of a
woman.

Drawing his revolver, the Colonel rushed to
the door near the altar, threw off the iron bar
and ran into the room.

CHAPTER VI

WHO SHOT ROSETTA?

Too FROZEN with fear to move, Judy and Susanne stared through the open doorway.

Colonel Thompson was looking incredulously around the small, square room. "There's no one here. There's not a soul in here." He pushed back his sun helmet and passed a hand across his moist forehead. "Can you beat that! By Jove, how could they have disappeared?"

"They must have gone out that door," Judy said. Then realizing that the outside door still was barred, she went on quickly, "No of course, they couldn't have gotten out that way. The noise did come from this room, didn't it?"

"Yes Judy, I'd have sworn the shot was fired in this room." Colonel Thompson was eyeing the narrow windows set high in the wall. They were mere slits, too narrow for any one to squeeze through.

Susanne said in a small, trembling voice, "It must have been a ghost."

Judy looked at her in disgust. "Don't talk so silly. You never heard of a ghost firing a gun, did you, Susanne? You do say the craziest things!"

"Now, now, don't scold," Colonel Thompson told her. "We thought the shot came from here and when we found no one, it was natural for Susanne to think of a ghost. A ghost is the only thing that could have disappeared from this room. But I'm sure it wasn't anything supernatural. Probably it was a drunken Indian celebrating close to the windows. When he fired off his gun, he frightened his companion and she screamed. That's about the whole story."

Susanne perked up, "See Judy, I'm not so silly after all. Every one knows the monastery's haunted, so it was logical for me to think that. It might have been a drunken Indian, but I still believe it was something else. The monastery is haunted, isn't it, Colonel Thompson?"

The Colonel smiled a bit. "That's what they say, Susanne. I don't believe in ghosts. But who knows if I'm right? You girls run along home now. I'll look around outside and see if I can locate the drunken Indian, or Susanne's hilarious spook."

As they watched him shut the door and replace the iron bar, Judy said, "Uncle Jim certainly did his best to make this chapel burglar proof. These doors have iron bars, and the outside one a high lock. Has anything ever been stolen before, Colonel Thompson?"

The Colonel shook his head. "No, not that I ever heard of, Judy. I too have had many a valuable thing stored in this old place. How the thief got in is a mystery—a mystery which may never be solved."

The girls followed him out of the dim, cool chapel into the glaring sunlight of the patio. Both glanced fearfully around, as they went to their horses, mounted and rode quickly through the archway and down the trail toward home.

All they thought of was getting away as far as possible before someone shot at them. "Oh boy! Every minute I expected that old, drunken Indian would pop at us," Judy said, bringing her galloping horse down to a trot and glancing back at the monastery.

Susanne was too far ahead to hear. Don Dexter was still galloping like fury. Scared as she was, Judy had to laugh. "Hi, Susanne! Hi there!" she called. "I'm talking to you!"

Susanne pulled up her horse and turned a frightened face to Judy. "I'm sure glad we're away from that old place," she gasped. "Oh my glory, talk about excitement! If anything more happens I'll just naturally pass out. Duck for that low limb, Judy!"

Judy ducked in the nick of time. "Yes, terrible things *have* sprung up. But Susanne, I'm worried about Colonel Thompson back there all alone. If only nothing happens to him."

With her riding crop, Susanne was brushing a huge fly off Don Dexter's brown, satiny neck. "Nothing must happen to him, Judy. It just mustn't!" For a moment she hesitated, then went on slowly, "And nothing must occur to Phil, either."

Judy did not say it aloud, but under her breath she was saying, "No, no, no harm must come to either one of them. We couldn't stand it if anything happened to them."

They were two anxious girls who waited for the Colonel. When he rode into the courtyard half an hour later, the girls rushed out to meet him.

"We were terribly worried about you!" Judy cried, "Oh Colonel Thompson we were so afraid you might be shot. I can't tell you how glad we are to see you!"

"You mustn't worry about me," the Colonel told them. "I'm as quick on the trigger as Dead-Eye-Dick. You've heard of that sharpshooter, haven't you? Sure you have. That's really who I am," he chuckled. "Well, if I'm not that fellow I'm as good a shot as he. Armed to the teeth, I went all around the outside of the monastery. Didn't find a soul. So I've come to the conclusion that it must have been a ghost, just as Susanne thought."

"Of course it was a ghost," Susanne laughed. "And I'm hoping we've seen the last of that old fellow. My goodness, look at your hand! I didn't dream the briars cut you like that. So that's the reason you had a handkerchief wrapped around it. You're letting us put some antiseptic on it, then you're staying for lunch."

The Colonel slipped his hand into the pocket of his linen riding coat. His hand was throbbing and paining very much. But he made light of it. The girls had been through enough without worrying about this. He insisted that it was nothing but a mere scratch that he would take care of it when he got back to camp. Another time he would remain for lunch.

The girls would not listen to it. So very shortly he was in a steamer chair on the broad corridor surrounding the courtyard and the girls were coming with hot water, gauze and iodine.

They looked so serious, the Colonel poked fun at them. "I admit this cut is deep, and jagged and rather horrid, but get that expression off your face. You look as though you expect me to lose my hand with blood poison, or something else equally fatal."

Blood poison! That's what the girls were fearing. They were thinking of what Marie had told them about touching the idol.

"Are you superstitious?" Judy asked. "We'd like to know for a special reason."

The Colonel asked quietly, "Who has been telling you things?" It was Judy who answered. "Marie told us that something is written under the gold hearts around the idol's neck. She said terrible things would happen to anyone touching the War God. Is it true, a curse is written there?"

The Colonel dipped his hand into the basin of hot water Susanne was holding. "Even if that were written underneath one of the hearts it's sheer nonsense to believe it," he answered evasively. "No curse can hurt one. Only ignorant, superstitious people believe in such things. Whew, this water is boiling hot, isn't it? But I can stand it. You girls are making a good job of taking care of this old hand of mine."

On the way to the monastery Judy had told him about telephoning the Stanton plantation and learning that Phil had gone up river. Now they were again discussing the boy.

"I don't think much of a father who would allow his son to go up in that wild section," Judy said wrathfully. "It is dangerous, isn't it?"

"It isn't exactly what one would call safe," he said gravely. "But perhaps Phil hasn't gone very far. The unfriendly Indians are miles up river. Phil is perfectly aware of this, so he will be wise enough to keep away from—"

Judy stuck the cork in the bottle of iodine and sprang to her feet. "Look over there! Something's happened! Something's happened!" she cried. "Someone's been hurt."

Two barefoot Indians were coming through the archway of the patio carrying someone on an improvised stretcher.

The Colonel got out of his chair. "By Jove something has happened!" he said in alarm. "Whom have you there?" he called in Spanish. "Who is it?"

"Señor, we do not know," one of the Indians replied. "We found this woman on the trail."

The three hurried down the flower-bordered path to where the men were carefully laying the stretcher on the grass. Judy and Susanne gasped in horror as they glimpsed the inert figure. It was Rosetta!

The two strange Indians were on their way up to the coffee picking section when they found her lying on the edge of the forest, along the trail. "I must get home. I must get home," she told them, then lapsed into unconsciousness.

Rosetta's gray hair was matted with blood and blood was oozing from a wound in her bare, right arm.

"Is she dying?" Judy asked in a trembling voice. "Oh Colonel Thompson, she mustn't die."

The Colonel was kneeling, his hand over Rosetta's heart. Then he made a hasty examination. "I don't believe she's dying, but she has been shot and is seriously wounded." He pulled a handkerchief from his pocket and wiped a smear of blood off his right hand.

Tears were rolling down Susanne's cheeks. "Where can we get a doctor? I'll telephone, if you tell me where to call."

"There's no doctor within fifty miles, Susanne," the Colonel told her. "But I've taken care of gunshot wounds before. We'll have her carried to her room, then I'll see what I can do."

He gave his orders in Spanish to the Indians. When Judy sensed the men were taking her out to the back courtyard, she ran after them calling, "No, no, not there. We want her taken up to the guest room next to ours."

"Up to a guest room? Do you believe your aunt would want you to do this?" the Colonel questioned. "Servants are kept in their own quarters, not given a guest room, my dear."

"Of course Aunt Alice won't mind," Judy insisted. "Rosetta's more than a servant, she's a member of the family. And she's hurt and must be where Susanne and I can take care of her. Call the men back. Tell them to carry her upstairs. Please, Colonel Thompson."

So up to a guest room Rosetta was carried. After she was gently lifted on the great, four-poster bed, Judy ran down to the kitchen after a kettle of boiling water, while Susanne brought gauze and antiseptic.

Colonel Thompson and the girls now realized that it was Rosetta they had heard scream when they were in the monastery. She had attempted to get home, had dragged herself over a very little used, but shorter trail, until loss of blood had made her unconscious. They were thankful the Indians had taken this trail on their way up to the coffee section.

After the wound on her scalp and arm had been dressed, the Colonel stood looking down at her. "I'm staying for awhile. I'm going to question her when she becomes conscious. I've been wondering if the man who shot her had anything to do with stealing the idol.   There may be some connection."

Susanne was putting the roll of unused gauze back into its box.   "What was she doing at the monastery, afraid as she is of ghosts?"

The Colonel nodded.   "Exactly.   That's what I desire to find out."

CHAPTER VII

"NO ONE SHOT ME, SEÑOR"

ROSETTA REGAINED consciousness in about an hour. To their amazement, she replied to the Colonel's question, "No one shot me, Señor."

Colonel Thompson touched her arm, "You have been shot, Rosetta. See, you have a bandage on your head and arm. You have been hurt. Don't you realize that?"

Rosetta closed her eyes and did not answer.

The Colonel went on in his patient, quiet voice, "You do know that you have been hurt. You can't help it, Rosetta, for you are in pain. Tell us who hurt you? Tell us, Rosetta?"

"Señor, no one hurt me," she replied in a low voice.

Susanne carefully brushed back a lock of Rosetta's gray hair. "Please try to understand what the Señor is asking you. Can't you remember that you were shot and tried to get home?"

The old Indian moved her head uneasily and murmured, "I tell you Señorita, no one shot me."

Colonel Thompson shoved his chair away from the bed and rose to his feet. "There's no use in questioning her any longer. If an Indian doesn't care to give information you can't drag it out of them. She knows his name, but she's not telling. I'll go back to the camp and return later on." He looked down at Rosetta who still had her eyes closed. "You're an obstinate, perverse old woman. You know well enough you've been shot. So you're not fooling me with your lies."

As he turned to leave the room, Judy placed her hand on his arm. "Wait a few minutes," she begged. "I want to try again. I'm sure her mind still is in a daze. I'm sure it is!" She knelt by the bed and covered Rosetta's hand with her own. "Are you listening? Rosetta, are you listening?"

Rosetta's eyes were still closed, but she nodded. "All right. Now, try to remember what happened. You have been shot. Can't you remember? You were down the trail and some one shot you."

"I know I've been shot, *Señorita*. I know," Rosetta whispered.

Judy looked up and smiled at the Colonel and Susanne. They smiled back at her. Judy again leaned over the sick woman. "Rosetta, when Susanne and I saw the men carry you in here all covered with blood, we felt so badly we cried.

We have done everything possible to make you comfortable, and we are going to take good care of you. We realize that whoever shot you didn't mean to do it. It was only an accident. So of course, we shan't punish him. But for a very special reason we must know who it was. Won't you please, tell us, Rosetta? Look at me."

Rosetta did not open her eyes and remained silent.

"Look at me, Rosetta," Judy whispered. "Look at me."

Slowly the woman raised her brown eyes. Her eyes were so full of pain, so beseeching, a lump came in Judy's throat.

"You're a dear. You're a dear, Rosetta. Bless your old loyal heart. You're shielding someone you love, aren't you. It's all right. We'll not bother you any more, Rosetta." She patted her lovingly, then rose to her feet.

They left the room and went down to the courtyard. Colonel Thompson was now absolutely convinced that the man who shot Rosetta had something to do with the theft, and that she was not only shielding him, but in some way might be involved.

When he told this to the girls Judy turned on him like a whirlwind.

"How dare you accuse her! She has lived with

Aunt Alice for twenty years and always has been loyal and faithful. Uncle Jim told me the other day that she would lay down her life for them, or to protect anything they valued. It's just as you said at the monastery; a drunken Indian shot off that gun and not for any reason except to celebrate. He shot Rosetta accidentally and she's afraid to tell for fear he'll be punished. You're wicked and cruel to accuse her. Don't you ever, ever do it again! I shan't—"

"Why Judy, what are you saying!" Susanne took hold of her arm. "Stop it, Judy. Stop talking like—"

Judy was rubbing a hand across her nose and glaring at the now quite red in the face Colonel. "I shan't stop it, Susanne. I'm sorry if I'm impertinent, Colonel Thompson, but Rosetta's lying up there hurt. She may die. You mustn't talk about her like that. I shan't have it!"

The Colonel's voice was brusque. "Sorry if I hurt you, Judy. But you must admit Rosetta is making it extremely difficult for me to believe she doesn't know something about this theft." He started across the courtyard to his horse. "I'll return later on. Perhaps she may feel more like talking then."

"If Phil comes, don't forget to question *him*," Judy called testily.

The Colonel looked back at the pretty girl standing by the balustrade and who still was gazing at him with hot, indignant eyes.

"Little pepper pot, you have a mighty big streak of loyalty," he told her. "But sometimes, loyalty can go too far. I'll not hurt that old woman, but I certainly intend to question her. As far as Phil is concerned that young man is going to have much to explain. I'll see to that."

When the Colonel disappeared through the archway of the patio Susanne said, "My glory, I wish you could have seen yourself! You were so furious your hair was standing on end and your face is still red as a lobster. For heaven's sake, can't you stand up for your friends without getting so wrathy?"

Judy sank on a chair and buried her face in her hands. "Not when they're sick and as good as Rosetta," she sobbed. "Oh Susanne, I'm so miserable. I'm so unhappy and worried about Rosetta, the idol and the curse—and everything."

Susanne's voice was full of sympathy. "I know you are, darling. And you're all worn out with the dreadful things you've been through. But we're going to forget all this for awhile. You lean back in that nice old easy chair and close your eyes. I'll lie down in the hammock. Smell the roses, Judy? It's like a bit of heaven out here, isn't it?"

Judy settled back in her chair and mopped her eyes. "Yes, it is heavenly in this lovely old patio. Perhaps I can go to sleep for a little while, Susanne. I'm going to try."

When the Colonel returned late that afternoon, the girls were relieved when he told them that he had decided not to question Rosetta. "It was foolish for me to consider it for even a moment," he said. "Knowing Indians as I do, I'm certain that no amount of pleading, or no threats will make her tell who shot her."

The bedroom of the plantation house opened up on a balcony which went around the second floor and faced the patio. The Colonel and the girls planned that Marie was to sleep outside of Rosetta's room on a cot and help take care of her.

The next morning Phil arrived. The girls were dressing Rosetta's arm and scalp wound when he came dashing into the courtyard on his handsome dapple gray horse.

It was Susanne who saw him first. "Oh Judy, he's come! Phil's here! Phil's here!" With the iodine bottle in her hand she was running across the room to the balcony.

Judy raced after her and grabbed her dress. "Come back here! Don't you dare go out there and call down to him. Don't you dare be polite!"

Susanne tried to pull away. "What's the matter with you! Of course, I'm going to tell him we're here. What's wrong about that?"

Judy still held her. "You're not calling down to him. He kept us waiting for two days. Now it's his turn. Let him cool his heels."

Susanne sighed and went back to the bed. "Oh Judy, you do get the craziest notions in that old head of yours. But all right, I'll give in." She rubbed her finger across a brown spot the iodine had splashed on her dress. "Just because you're so hot headed I've ruined my skirt, and Phil's down there wondering where we are."

Judy's face was grim as she took a pair of scissors from the stand and cut off a strip of gauze. "I'm sorry you got splashed. But after the way he's acted we're not letting him think we're crazy to see him. Haven't you any pride, Susanne?" she asked sternly.

Susanne flushed. "Certainly I have. I didn't think, that's all. You're right, Judy. It's just as well to make him wait."

"I'm glad you have come to your senses," Judy told her, as she wrapped gauze around Rosetta's arm. "Come on, Susanne, I need your help now."

Susanne eyed Judy fearfully as she sat on the

bed and placed her finger on the bandage to hold it tight while Judy gave it a neat turn. She was thinking that it was the thing to do to make Phil wait, but she dreaded to have Judy scold him. She was afraid Judy might if Phil didn't explain why he hadn't gone riding with them.

"Oh darling don't be cross and make a scene." She smiled at Judy. "You know you have a fierce temper when you get riled up. I have too. But it doesn't pay to fly off the handle. It never gets you anywhere."

"It gives you a heap of satisfaction," Judy's face was grim, as she again wrapped the cloth about Rosetta's arm. "We promised not to mention the idol. I shan't. But if he doesn't explain why he broke that engagement with us to go riding, he'll hear plenty from me."

"Oh Judy, you're terrible," Susanne said nervously. "Phil's off his horse and looking around for us. No one's down there. So I reckon he's wondering where the servants and we are."

"Stop stretching your neck and looking out of that window," Judy scolded. "Let him wonder where we are. What do I care. You pay attention to what you're doing. Put your finger up higher on the bandage. That's right. Well, we're almost through, so soon you'll be seeing your precious old Phil."

Susanne was so nervous over what might happen that on the way down stairs again she pleaded with Judy. "Don't jump on him right off. Try to keep calm and be kind. Even if you don't like his excuse, if you don't believe him, don't make a scene." She went on brightly. "Do you know something, Judy? I bet anything you were right when you said that he may have gone up river to bring back a surprise for us. Oh Judy, I feel sure that's just what he did."

Judy was as nervous as Susanne. Her heart was thumping like a trip hammer, but outwardly, she was calm. She was hoping desperately that Phil might be able to explain. But like a dam, back of this intense longing, was a torrent of wrath ready to descend upon him if he failed to explain things satisfactorily. That he might have gone up river to bring back a surprise for them seemed now a crazy thought of hers.

Susanne was begging again, "Don't be cross with him, Judy. Please, don't be cross."

Judy said calmly, "Don't worry. I'll be nice and give him a chance. And I'll try to keep my temper, darling. I'll try hard to keep it."

CHAPTER VIII

They found Phil in the open corridor which surrounded the patio. He was standing by a table, idly turning the pages of a magazine. When he saw them he broke into a broad grin and with a loud clanking of spurs, hurried down to greet them.

"Hi there! I was beginning to think this place was deserted. The top of the morning to you!" he said gaily.

"Hello, Phil! I'm glad to see you," Judy told him. It was not necessary for her to make her voice sound happy. The sight of him was giving her an unexpected thrill, a very real joy.

"I'm glad to see you too," Susanne laughed. "We missed you like everything. But don't get conceited over that. The reason we missed you is because you're the only boy we're acquainted with down here."

Phil's brown eyes danced, "Gosh, I have sense enough to know that. I'm sure lucky to be the only guy for miles and miles. I don't give a hoot why you missed me, the big thing is you were so lonesome for me you pined away. Both of you look positively skinny. But never mind, I'll not leave you again." He quit his foolishness, the smile left his face as he went on soberly, "Sorry I had to disappoint you about the ride, but it couldn't be helped."

Susanne sat on the balustrade. "That's all right. We didn't mind at all, Phil. Really we didn't."

Phil looked surprised and pleased. "I'm sure glad to hear you say that. It worried me like blazes to run off the way I did. But honest, I had to go." He eyed Judy admiringly. "You're looking mighty swell this morning. That pale blue dress makes your complexion look more pink and white than ever." In his excitement, he had blurted that out. Embarrassed, even his ears became red. He looked away for a moment, then said quickly, "Do you want to go on our postponed ride to the second river this morning?"

Susanne slid off the balustrade, "We'd love to," she said enthusiastically. "But we can't ride for more than an hour. We're helping take care of Rosetta. You didn't know that she was found on the trail with two bullet wounds, did you?"

Phil was standing with his hands in his pockets staring at her. "For the love of Pete!" he gasped. "How in the dickens did that happen? Have you found out who did it? Is she dangerously hurt?"

Judy told him about the two Indians finding her on the trail. She never mentioned the monastery, nor the shots Colonel Thompson, Susanne and she had heard down there. Mentioning the temple might bring up the subject of the idol. She had promised the Colonel not to say a word about that.

Phil was all sympathy, and indignant over the fact that some one had shot Rosetta. "Sure it was a drunken Indian," he said. "No one else would shoot at her. They all know she's one of the swellest Indians on the plantation. I'm glad she's no worse off than she is. The old fool might have killed her. Well, if we're going for a ride, get into your other duds. I'm going to take you on a new trail this morning. You'll see alligators and lions and giraffes and elephants and—"

Susanne laughed. "Ain't it ducky we're going to see all them animals! We'll be ready in a jiffy. Come on, Judy."

"Wait a minute," Judy took hold of Susanne's hand. "Wait a minute, honey." Phil had not told them why he had gone up river. He had not explained anything. She was cruelly disappointed. She could not stand it. She had to make him clear himself. "Why did you go up river, Phil?" she asked gently. "Why did you break our engagement?"

"Why?" Phil nervously ran his finger around his shirt collar. Then he answered flippantly, "Oh because I had to go up river on important business. I told you I was sorry as the dickens to disappoint you, but honestly, it couldn't be helped."

Susanne was gripping Judy's hand and begging, "Come on, Judy. Please don't say anything more. Please."

Judy ignored her. She eyed Phil soberly, "Why?" she questioned. "Why couldn't it be helped?"

A red flame spread over Phil's face. But he smiled, in spite of his evident embarrassment. "Because I'm a big business man, Judy. Had a very important matter to attend to. Too important to tell little girls. Gosh, I didn't know you were so curious."

Judy drew a long breath. She had been hoping that the reason he hadn't explained right off was because he hadn't considered it necessary, that he thought it too unimportant. Now, she realized that deliberately, he was keeping the reason from them. Hurt and angry, she went over to a table, picked up a newspaper and seating herself, began to read.

"Judy, aren't you going riding?" Susanne asked. "Come on. We both need to get away from the house for a little while. A ride will do us a lot of good."

Judy did not answer.

Phil's face brightened. He dug his hand into his hip pocket and brought out two narrow, green leather belts. "One of our Indians makes these and I thought that perhaps you girls might like them," he said handing one to Susanne.

Susanne gave a squeal of delight. "Oh it's beautiful! It's perfectly darling!" she cried, eyeing it admiringly. "It's so gay and lovely, with its silver studding and gorgeous silver buckle. You're a dear to give it to me, Phil. Thanks, thanks a million!"

Phil beamed, "Glad you like it. I think they're mighty pretty myself." He pulled off the elastic band which was keeping the other belt in a neat roll, allowed it to fall its full length, then carried it over to Judy. "Here's one for you, Judy," he said, holding it out to her.

Judy continued to read her newspaper.

"Say, what in heck's wrong with you? You're not cross at me for something, are you? Don't you want this?" He held it up for her inspection. "Look at it, Judy," he said in a coaxing voice. "I think it's mighty nifty."

Judy glanced up at him. "Do you know that the jade idol's gone, that someone has stolen it from the chapel?"

"Yes, I heard about it. It broke me all up, Judy."

Judy raised her eyebrows, "Oh, you did know it, did you? Well, I should think if it upset you so much, you would have talked about it the minute you got here."

It was not only this remark, but something in her tone, which made him bristle a little. But he kept his voice calm as he said, "I didn't say anything because I didn't know whether you girls had heard it. I didn't want to be the one to make you feel badly, so I waited for you to say something. I can't for the life of me understand how the thief got the idol out of the chapel."

"Can't you? That's strange."

"Just what do you mean by that, Judy?" he demanded sharply. "What do you mean?"

"I mean," Judy laid the newspaper on the table. "I mean that you didn't lock the door, that it was left unlocked on purpose."

Horrified, Susanne swooped down and covered

Judy's mouth with her hand. "Don't say that! Please, please! You mustn't say that. Take it back, Judy. Take it—"

Pushing Susanne aside, Judy sprang to her feet, her eyes blazing.

"If you didn't leave the door open on purpose, if you didn't take the idol, tell us why you didn't stay and go riding with us! And explain why you started up river two hours after we had you down at the monastery!"

Phil's face went white. "So that's it. You— you believe I am the thief."

Almost beside herself, Susanne rushed over to him and placed her hand on his arm, "Please, explain why you went away," she begged. "Judy likes you so much she doesn't wish to believe anything bad about you. I told her you could clear yourself, that you could explain everything."

Phil said slowly, "I didn't take the idol, and I'm certain I snapped the padlock. You girls will have to believe me guilty, if you feel like it, for I'm not telling why I went up river, and I'm not telling why I didn't go riding that morning." He turned to Judy, "As for you, you're a mean, little pin-headed nothing! That's what you are! You go to blazes!"

He raced over to his horse, mounted and went galloping out of the courtyard.

"Oh Judy, how could you say that!" Susanne cried. "How could you accuse him of taking the idol. That was a terrible, terrible, thing to do."

Weak and shaken, Judy stared at the archway through which Phil had disappeared. "But Susanne, he wouldn't explain," she said in a trembling voice, "I gave him a chance, and he wouldn't tell why he went up river." Suddenly, it came to her that she had broken her promise to Colonel Thompson. She had promised not to mention the idol to Phil. She had not only talked about it, but had accused him of being the thief. Overwhelmed by what she had done, she sank on a chair and said in consternation, "Susanne, what will Colonel Thompson say! I've broken my word to him!"

Susanne felt sorry for her, but not enough to hide her displeasure over the way Judy had acted. "You mean all right, Judy," she said to her. "But you fly off and say such frightful things. I'll bet Colonel Thompson will be furious with you. You deserve it. And you deserved what Phil said to you. No one has any right to accuse a person of being a thief, unless she knows positively that he is. If you had been a boy, he'd have knocked you down."

Judy pulled a handkerchief out of a sleeve of her dress and savagely blew her nose. "I'm so

cross at myself! I don't see why I flare up the
way I do. I haven't any sense when I get cross.
I forget everything, but what I'm saying. I deserved everything Phil and you said to me."

"You certainly did," Susanne agreed. Judy
was looking so desperately unhappy, so crushed,
Susanne told her, "Oh cheer up, Judy. Colonel
Thompson won't hang you. It isn't so serious
after all. He'll understand how you happened to
say what you did to Phil. He'll forgive you. So
quit worrying about that. Do you know something?" she grinned. "You have a rotten temper
and can't be trusted, and there are a million other
things wrong with you. Why we all love you, I
don't know. But everyone does, Judy. So don't
look so glum."

Susanne's face clouded. All the time Judy was
going for Phil, Marie was standing under the rose
arbor. She had heard the whole thing. No
doubt she would tell all over the place that Judy
had accused Phil of stealing the idol. She considered saying something to Marie, then decided
that the best thing to do was to leave it alone, not
even to mention it to Judy.

After persuading Judy to lie down in a hammock, Susanne ran into the house, brought out
her stationery, dragged a large chair close to Judy
and began to write a letter home.

It was quiet in the patio. There was no sound save the water splashing in the moss-rimmed basin of the fountain, and Tito on his perch, talking softly to himself in Spanish.

Judy lay there thinking of Phil. She firmly believed him guilty. If he were not, what reason would there be for not telling why he had left them at the monastery, why he had gone up river? There couldn't possibly be any other reason. She was sorry that she had broken her word, that she had said anything to Phil about the idol. But she was more sorry she had discovered that it was Phil who was the thief. Tears welled in her eyes. How could he have done such a thing! she wondered miserably. How could a grand boy like Phil do such a heart breaking thing!

She watched Pedro trot down the corridor and disappear into the hall which led upstairs. Then Judy's thoughts turned to Rosetta, who was again having a high fever. It occurred to Judy that they could do something to make her feel more comfortable.

She raised herself on her elbow, "Susanne, let's give Rosetta an alcohol rub," she said eagerly. "She's burning up with fever and so restless, it might make her feel better. Mother put a bottle of alcohol in my trunk. I'll go up and look for it, in a few minutes."

Susanne waved a sheet of paper to dry the ink. "That's a good idea, Judy. When I finish this letter I'll go up and give her the rub myself. You lie still and rest."

Judy settled down on her hammock. "No, I'll go with you," she told her. "And don't break your neck trying to get that letter finished. There isn't any particular hurry."

In a few minutes, Pedro appeared and came toward them holding something in his hand. "I gave Rosetta one of these and I have one for you," he said, handing both girls a string of gray stones.

"What on earth is this?" Susanne asked, examining it curiously. "Can't you see? It's a necklace," Judy told her, holding hers up and eyeing it admiringly. "It's lovely of you, Pedro. I've never seen anything like these little, round, flat stones. They're beautiful."

Susanne was turning her stones over and over, "Yes, they are beautiful. And look, Judy, every little stone has a faint white line around the center of it. How could anyone find so many little stones alike! Pedro this will be a grand souvenir for us to take home. Thank you, so much, Pedro. Thank you, a lot."

"They are wind stones. Magic stones, they are," Pedro told them, smiling. "Señoritas, you wear them and they will keep away evil spirits."

Judy slipped her string over her head. "You're an old darling to get this for us, Pedro," she said, smiling up at the weazened old fellow. "I'm sure no harm can come to us now. Do you know what Aunt Alice told us over the telephone last night? She said she knows you and Rosetta will take good care of us while she is away, so she's not worrying at all any more."

Pedro's black eyes twinkled and he smiled broadly. "The *Señora*, she say that? I am very happy. *Gracias, Señorita. Gracias.* I am very glad the *Señora* has not heard what has happened since she went away. I want to take good care of you, and the wind stones, they will help. I go now." They watched the old Indian as he went on his little dog trot down the flower bordered path and disappeared into the back courtyard.

"Isn't he a darling! He's about the swellest thing I know," Judy said fervently.

"He sure is swell," Susanne agreed. "He's doing his best to look after us. Bless his old heart! These little stones must be hard to find. I bet the old fellow's been collecting them for years. And to think he gave them to us! Well, I hope his little old charms will keep evil away. Do you know what you're going to do, Judy?" she asked, folding her letter and slipping it into an envelope. "Little Judy's going to lie right here and rest, while Susanne gives Rosetta her bath."

Judy wouldn't hear to it. She slid out of her hammock and started to go through strenuous exercises. "Hi, look at me. I'm so full of pep I could give Rosetta a dozen baths," she laughed. "Anyway, you never can find anything. So how could you find a bottle tucked away in a lot of clothes." She grabbed Susanne's hand. "Come on, darling. I'll let you help."

Up in their room Judy was on her knees searching through her trunk when Susanne stooped down and picked up a silver bar pin set with blue-green aquamarine. It belonged to her. She hadn't worn it since she had come to Mexico. Wondering how it happened to be on the floor, she hurried over to their bureau and pulled open the small drawer in which she kept her jewelry. The drawer was empty. Every piece was gone.

"My jewelry's gone," she cried frantically. "Oh Judy, a thief has taken my necklace, bead chains, my watch, every bit of jewelry I have!" She jerked open one of the large drawers and began pawing through her silk underwear and other things. "Every bit of it's gone, Judy!"

Judy came tearing across the room, "It couldn't be, Susanne. Are you sure?"

"Oh yes, I'm sure." Susanne's voice was high

pitched, hysterical. "I knew they weren't in this drawer, but had to look. Oh Judy, my watch, my necklaces, bracelets, everything has been stolen."

Judy pulled open the small drawer belonging to herself and looked in. "Mine are here. Nothing of mine has been touched. Oh I'm so sorry for you, honey. I'm dreadfully sorry for you. Do you suppose it was Marie? She's the only one I can think of who—"

Susanne's face was livid with fury, as she shoved in the drawer and sprang to her feet. "Yes, it was Marie who stole them. She's a mean, contemptible sneak thief, that's what she is! You watch me get my things back. I'll show her!"

Judy grabbed her. "Wait, Susanne, wait!" she said in a low, tense voice. "You mustn't make a scene in Rosetta's room. She's too sick. I'll call Marie to come in here."

Marie came in. As usual, she was looking very pretty, very happy and smiling.

"You want me, Señorita?" she asked, in her soft little voice. Startled by Judy's and Susanne's angry expression, she stopped, glanced from one to the other. "What is wrong, Señoritas? What have I done?" she questioned soberly.

Susanne rushed over to her and grabbed her by the arms. "I'll show you what's wrong! You miserable little thief! You give me back my watch and other things you stole from my drawer. Hear me! You run and get them as fast as your legs will carry you!"

Marie's black eyes were wide with fright. "Let me go! Let me go, *Señorita!*" She tried to break away. "I did not take your jewelry. I am no thief! Let me go!"

Susanne was now shaking her. "I'll not let you go until you tell me what you did with my watch and bracelets and other things. Tell me! You hear me, Marie! You tell me what you did with them!"

Judy had never seen Susanne like this. Susanne, always so mild and sweet, was now like a wild woman.

Judy put her arm around her. "Stop it, Susanne! Please, listen to me. Stop shaking her and yelling! You'll not get anywhere, acting like this. Stop shaking her and listen to me. You're acting like a crazy person. You're frightening her so terribly, she'll never own up. Let go of her, please? Please?"

Susanne let go of Marie's arms and turned on Judy. "All right. All right. You're so smart, see what you can do," she stormed. "You get back my jewelry. Go on! Do it! Do it!"

Realizing she was free, Marie started to run. Judy stopped her. Marie backed against the wall, tears streaming down her cheeks.

Judy placed her hand on the girl's shoulder. "Listen to me," she said in a calm, gentle voice. "Miss Susanne's jewelry is not in her drawer. Some one has taken it. You were the only person up here, so of course, it was you, Marie. We know you love pretty things. That isn't anything against you. But you shouldn't have taken, I mean, borrowed Miss Susanne's watch and necklace and bracelets, without asking her permission. Now be a good girl and bring them back. You'll not be punished, and I promise you on my word of honor, we'll not tell a soul about this." She smiled at her, "You're going to do it, aren't you, Marie?"

"I did not take them," Marie sobbed. "I tell you I did not take them. Please, Señorita, let me go! Let me go!" They pleaded and threatened, but Marie continued to protest she did not know where the jewelry was, that she had not taken the watch, bracelets and other things.

At last they gave up in despair. "Very well, you may go," Susanne told her. "But don't for a minute think you're getting out of this. We're going to catch you, and you'll be punished for what you've done. You're a little old sneak thief. Get out of here! Beat it!"

Marie held out both hands. "Do not tell anyone you say I stole," she pleaded. "They will believe it, and I shall want to die."

Susanne hesitated. What difference would it make? If she consented, perhaps Marie might decide to confess. "All right, we'll not tell," she said. "But remember, now, that you haven't owned up, so when we do catch you, every one for miles around will know what a thief you are. Go on back to Rosetta. It's time for her medicine." She waved her hand. "Go on! Get out of here!"

Like a frightened rabbit, Marie scurried out of the room. Judy sank on her bed. "Whew, if this hasn't been some day!" she gasped. "I accused Phil of being a thief and now you accused Marie. They are two miserable specimens, aren't they!" Her voice was full of contempt. Silence for a moment, then she added with a chuckle, "And we are two smart girls, Susanne."

Susanne was gazing out of the window. "Oh Judy, I don't know. Maybe we are and maybe not. Perhaps we're not as smart as we think we are," she said slowly.

CHAPTER IX

By three o'clock, Rosetta was much worse. She had a high fever and was delirious. Judy was filling an ice bag and Susanne was on her knees bathing Rosetta's face with alcohol, when Colonel Thompson entered the room.

"Hello, girls? How is she?" His voice showed his anxiety, as he hurried over to the bed.

The girls were tremendously relieved to see him. Judy told him that Rosetta was very sick. The thermometer was broken so they were unable to take her temperature. "But we know her fever is very high," she told him. "Put your hand on her face, and you'll see how ill she is."

The Colonel leaned over the sick woman and placed his hand on her forehead. "By George you're right," he said gravely. "I'll send Pedro over to my camp after a different antiseptic, also a bottle of spirits of nitre. Is the old fellow around?"

The girls knew he was in the back courtyard mending a saddle. But it was not medicine from Colonel Thompson's camp Susanne wanted for Rosetta. It was a physician like their dear old

Doctor Bagley at home, who would come in carrying his little black bag and looking so cheerful, so experienced and capable, that anyone knew he would make his patient well.

She put the cork in the bottle of alcohol and set it on the table. "Pedro's in the back courtyard," she told him. "I'll run down and give him your message. But Colonel Thompson, instead of sending after medicine, try to get a doctor. Won't you please?" Susanne's lips were quivering and she was trying hard to keep back the tears. "Rosetta's terribly ill. She must have a doctor. Please send for one," she begged.

The Colonel felt the need of a physician for Rosetta as much as Susanne. He felt the need desperately. But the girls were far too worried for him to show his own uneasiness.

He said briskly, "My dear, I'd get a doctor if it were possible. But I explained before that there isn't one within fifty miles. So you see, it's up to me to look after Rosetta. Of course, I can do it," he smiled at the girls, and went on reassuringly. "Down here where we haven't a doctor, we have to know how to take care of our sick Indians. So don't worry, we'll pull Rosetta through this illness. We'll have her well in no time. I'll go down myself and tell Pedro what I want him to bring. When I come up, I'll have a look at

Rosetta's arm and see what is causing this trouble."

When the Colonel returned and lifted the compress off the wound, the girls gave a gasp of horror. Pus was oozing out of it and it was inflamed and angry looking. Judy raced down to the kitchen after boiling water, and soon they were helping the Colonel cleanse the putrid sore, putting on the antiseptic they had on hand, making it do until Pedro came back to the camp.

Again and again Susanne wanted to telephone their aunt, but Colonel Thompson insisted that they were doing everything possible for Rosetta and that Aunt Alice was needed far more by her sick friend than here at home.

Until eight o'clock in the evening, they worked on the sick woman. Not until then, when her temperature begin to fall did they consider her out of danger.

Then they went down to the moonlit patio where Colonel Thompson wearily stretched himself out in a steamer chair and took out his pipe. Susanne was sitting near by drinking a tall limeade. Judy stood by the fountain trying to muster up sufficient courage to tell Colonel Thompson what she had done; to confess to him that not only had she talked to Phil about the idol, but had accused him of stealing it. Many times during the day she wanted to tell him but shame had held her back. Now she had to. She stood there looking at the sparkling water splashing into the moss rimmed basin, and tried desperately to think of a way to begin.

To her relief it was the Colonel who brought up the subject of Phil. He remarked casually, "Well, our young man hasn't returned yet, has he? But don't worry girls, I'm quite certain he'll show up tomorrow, and will have some interesting things to tell you about this sudden trip of his."

Judy turned, "He was here this morning, Colonel Thompson. I did something I'm very much ashamed of," she said in a low voice.

The Colonel rammed more tobacco into his pipe and smiled at her. "Scolded him for running away, did you? Well, he merited it all right. More power to you, Judy!"

Judy was thinking miserably, I'd give a million dollars if that was all I did say. She drew a long breath. "I scolded him. But that isn't what I am talking about. I accused him of stealing the idol."

Colonel Thompson thundered, "*You accused him of stealing it?* What right had you to do that? And didn't you promise me on your word of honor not to mention the idol?"

Judy nodded. "Yes, I did," her eyes were beseeching his forgiveness. "Truly, I didn't mean to."

"Well, why did you?" he questioned sharply. "Why did you break your word?"

"Because he didn't tell why he went up river, and when I asked he refused to explain. I was so furious it just slipped out. I'm sorry I broke my word. I'm terribly sorry."

Tears were in Judy's eyes. She looked miserable and penitent. Susanne leaned forward and covered the Colonel's hand with her own. "Please don't be cross with her. She told you she's sorry."

The Colonel's gray eyes did not soften. He had met Judy's kind before; a magnetic leader, but one whose impulsiveness and quick temper were forever getting her into trouble. A person too, who was so pretty and had such an appealing way that always she was forgiven.

Now she had broken her word, something which to him was unthinkable. He had planned to question Phil. He knew the boy wouldn't refuse to give him some sort of answer. Then he would have pinned him down. Now Phil was accused of taking the idol; if he were innocent, he might be too incensed to tell anything; if guilty, too wary. He was sorry about that, but more important was the fact that Judy had broken her word.

He said to Judy, "One always accepts an apology, but I am not very proud of you. Remember; a thoroughbred does not break her word. Well, enough of this. What did Phil say? What was his reaction?"

It was all Judy could do to keep back the tears. "He swore he didn't take it," she said. "But he wouldn't explain why he couldn't go riding with us, or why he had to go home after we had taken him down there and shown him the idol."

"He'll tell me, or I'll know the reason why," the Colonel said brusquely. Both Susanne and Judy were looking so depressed he softened a bit. "Before I leave will you mind giving me a little music?" he asked. "Not anything sad. I think we all need something lively to cheer us up."

It was difficult for him to keep his face straight at their change of expression. Susanne flew into the house after Judy's guitar. Judy, all smiles, said, "We couldn't possibly sing any other kind tonight. Do you know why?"

"Of course I know. Rosetta's better."

"Yes and because I think you've partly forgiven me and for another reason. Guess!"

He thought for a moment. "You girls were

worried about my hand. It's improving, so probably that's it."

Judy nodded. "And there's still another reason. Can't you guess?" The Colonel shook his head. "Haven't the least idea. I give up."

Leaning forward on her chair Judy said breathlessly, "Because of the idol. I was scared that the curse had something to do with your sore hand and Rosetta's sickness. I knew Rosetta hadn't touched the old thing, but she's a member of the household. I was—"

The Colonel broke in sharply, "Stop talking such drivel! I'm astonished at you. The reason those words are underneath the hearts is because no one but the priests were permitted to touch a War God. I'm quite sure that is the reason for the curse being there. It doesn't mean a thing! How under heavens can a piece of jade hurt any one? Cut out such talk, Judy."

I know the War God is only a piece of jade," Judy admitted. "And I've tried hard to make myself believe there isn't anything to that curse. But I keep thinking of Rosetta being shot and your sore hand, and of the terrible things that happened to the men who opened the tomb of King Tut. Every blessed man who had anything to do with the opening of that tomb died a horrible death. You know they did, Colonel Thompson."

The Colonel informed her that not a single man had died a tragic death and that several were still hale and hearty. "Simply newspaper talk, Judy. It made a good story." He eyed her gravely. "Get this nonsense out of your head. It isn't good to think of such things. You promise me to never bring this up again. *And this time keep your promise!*"

Judy was not convinced that there wasn't something to that curse or the one on the jade idol, but she readily agreed not to bring up the subject, ever.

The next morning Rosetta's temperature was normal. The Colonel telephoned, and learning the good news, did not come over. The girls had a quiet, restful time until the evening and then, THEY SAW THE GHOST!

The moonlight again flooded the patio with its soft, silvery light and in the air lay the fragrance of lilies and roses. Susanne almost asleep, was lying in a hammock on the open piazza facing the courtyard. Judy curled up in a large, wicker chair, gazed at the water as it splashed and sparkled into the moss-rimmed basin of the fountain. She then turned her glance on the sparkling water of the lily pool built beneath a large orange

tree along the stone wall of the patio, near the
entrance to the back courtyard. In it swam a
family of gold fish which Judy had promised to
tend. It came to her with a start that she had
neglected them for two days. Telling Susanne
what she was going to do, she hurried into the
house, brought out the box of food and was running across the patio when *it* appeared!

It stood at the entrance to the back courtyard;
a specter in white with gaping cavities for eyes
and a grinning, toothless mouth. She caught
only a glimpse of his skeleton-like arms as she
whirled and went screaming up to the house.

Susanne also had spied it before it suddenly
vanished; she too, shook with hysterical sobs.
Pedro and Marie hastened in from the servants'
quarters.

"A ghost! Oh, Pedro, I saw the ghost!" Judy
cried. "It was horrible! I'm so frightened, so
frightened."

In spite of the fact that both girls declared it
was at the entrance to the back courtyard, Pedro
and Marie had not seen it.

"You must have seen it, for it was right there,"
Susanne said, pointing to the place. "I saw it too,
and it was right there."

"You poor *Señoritas*," Marie leaned down and
patted Susanne. "You go away from here. I

take care of Rosetta. You go where *Señora* is. There no ghosts can hurt you."

That's exactly what Judy and Susanne wanted to do. They would leave in the morning. They couldn't stand any more terrifying experiences, any more ghosts or burglars prowling around their room. They had to be with their aunt where they would feel safe and secure.

But in the morning they talked it over, and decided that it would be an imposition for two strange girls to go to a home where a woman was seriously ill. Then too, they would have to tell their aunt what had happened and it would upset her dreadfully. As far as the ghost was concerned, there was no doubt in their mind but what they had seen one, but their common sense told them a ghost, no matter how horrible, couldn't possibly harm them. It was up to them to stay right here and do all they could to find the idol. That was their job.

Marie was disturbed over their decision. "If you stay something terrible might happen to you," she told them. "You should go where there are no ghosts."

Indians are very superstitious, even old Pedro begged the girls to leave. But his and Marie's pleadings were to no avail; the girls were not leaving the plantation.

Rosetta continued to improve. She was so much better when Colonel Thompson telephoned after lunch he urged the girls to go for a ride. "Rosetta doesn't need your attention any longer," he told them. "From now on, Marie can take entire charge of her. A ride in the forest will do you a world of good."

The trail through the wood was cool and fragrant and it was so wonderful to be on a horse again that they rode for more than two hours.

They were returning on the trail which led through the coffee picking section, when they heard excited shouts and yells. A man darted out of the deep thicket of coffee trees with a mob in pursuit. He was almost up to the girls before he was caught. Carlos, the overseer, seized the fellow, and started to cuff him about.

"Señoritas! Señoritas!" he called. "Here is a thief. I have a thief."

Riding up to the edge of the crowd Judy called, "Have you the idol? Oh Carlos, did you get back the idol?"

"No, Señorita, but I have a thief." Still clutching the fellow's arm, Carlos reached in his pocket and brought out two narrow gold bracelets. "I saw this coffee picker give these to his girls. I know he stole them somewhere. Are they yours?"

Susanne was eagerly reaching down for them. "They're mine." She slipped them on her arm and patted the shining gold circles. "Thank you for getting them for me. Oh I'm so happy. He stole five others just like these together with some bead chains and a little ball watch. Please try to get them back for me. Please, Carlos."

Carlos glared at his prisoner and roared out a torrent of Spanish. The young fellow muttered something and stared straight ahead.

Carlos shrugged his shoulders. "He say he found them on the trail near the monastery. He say he know nothing about idol or anything else. He a bad hombre. Many times he steal and cut with knife. He no good." A sudden thought struck him. He clapped his hands and shouted to the Indian to turn his face up to the girls. Slowly the Indian did as he was commanded. "Señoritas, you look at him hard," Carlos told them. "Is this the man who climbed up to your room and stole the key?"

For only a moment did Susanne look at the cruel face, at the shifting black eyes, at the jagged scar down the right cheek. Could this man be the one who had climbed up to their room? Again, all the terror of that night swept over her and she felt sick and weak. She put her hands across her eyes and cried, "I don't know. I'm not sure. But take him away. Take him away, please!"

Two Indians were tying the fellow's hands behind his back while Judy was saying, "Listen honey, I don't believe this is the man. Anyway, if he is, he can't hurt you now. Don't you think the one who came up to our room was taller and more slender?"

She told Carlos they had not caught sight of the man's face. They had seen him only in the shadow of the post and as he raced across their room. It seemed to her that this fellow was not as tall as the other, but she was not sure.

"You go now, Señoritas," Carlos said. "I attend to this fellow. I get the things he stole. Adiós, Señoritas. Adiós!"

Riding down to the house Judy said, "I'm glad you have two of your bracelets. If he stole your jewelry, I'm sure he's the one who stole the key and the idol."

Susanne was conscience stricken because they had accused Marie. She would try to make amends by giving her a present of some kind. But after talking it over, they were not so certain the maid did not take the jewelry. She had a better chance than this Indian, and after all, this fellow might be telling the truth about finding the bracelets on the trail. Marie could have lost them there.

They left their horses in the corral and walked up to the house. In the patio, Tito the parrot, was pacing up and down on his perch calling, "Hello! Hello!" Susanne eyed him a bit wistfully. "I know it sounds crazy," she said, "but I wish both of us were birds, then we wouldn't be in all this mess."

Judy grinned. "You're right. This minute I'd rather be anything than myself, even a cow. But we're not. We are two girls in a mess of trouble."

They had a shower and were getting into thin, cool dresses, when a knock sounded at the door.

It was Marie. A very excited Marie and she was saying with glowing eyes, "I have news for you, Señoritas. I think I know where the idol is."

"You do?" Judy cried. "Where is it, Marie?"

"Up river in a cave." Marie's voice was almost a whisper.

Susanne asked, "How do you know? Who told you?"

Marie nervously fingered the red rose in her hair. "Ricardo told me, Señorita. He came up from coffee picking and just told me. He told me where Master Phil went." She went on eagerly, "You think Master Phil stole the idol, don't you? I heard you talking to him. I—"

Susanne broke in, "She doesn't know anything of the kind. You mustn't repeat that, Marie."

Judy was thinking that perhaps Marie was glad to accuse someone of stealing, because she herself was under suspicion of taking Susanne's jewelry. She said with dignity, "Miss Susanne is telling the truth, Marie. I really don't know who took the idol. Where is the cave?"

"I told you up river. Up a branch of *El Negro*."

Judy eyed her suspiciously. Marie was flighty, irresponsible. She didn't know whether to believe her or not. She asked, "How does Ricardo know where the cave is?"

Marie explained an Indian who lived up river came down to help with the coffee picking. He told Ricardo he had seen Phil up at the cave. The Indian did not know that Phil had carried the idol up river.

Judy decided it did sound plausible. It was true that Marie had overheard her accusing Phil of taking the idol up river. It would be natural for Phil to hide it in a cave. But Judy was wondering why Marie was telling them instead of hurrying to Colonel Thompson with the good news, for if the idol were in the cave Marie could claim the reward.

She asked the girl this. Marie explained quickly, "Ricardo and I knew you would like to surprise the *Señor* and get it back yourselves."

She smiled a little. "And anyway, you would give us the money."

The girls laughed. Judy said, "You're a great one. You want us to do the work and give you and Ricardo the reward. But you know well enough we can't go up there. It's too wild and dangerous. So you and Ricardo will have to go after all."

Marie told them that the cave was not up in the wild section. "A little river branches off *El Negro*," she said. "Ricardo does not know this river, but José does. He will be glad to take you, Señorita."

Judy too, felt José would be glad to take them and it would be wonderful to get back the idol. But she would rather have Pedro go with them. "Pedro knows this section too, doesn't he?" she asked.

Marie shook her head. "No, no, you must not say anything to Pedro," she protested vigorously. "Pedro knows the country, but he is old and queer. He would say you must not go off the plantation." She clasped and unclasped her hands. "Please do not let him know you are going. José is good. He will take care of you. Pedro is over at the Lacaya plantation. You must be gone before he comes home."

More than anything in the world Judy wanted

to find the idol. Here was her chance! It was a little after four o'clock. If they hurried, they could get away before Pedro returned.

She turned to Susanne. "We're going! Let's hunt up José and get started before Pedro finds out about it. We'll have to hurry! Come on, Susanne!"

Susanne stood still. "We're not running off like this. We're waiting until tomorrow. We're telling Colonel Thompson and he'll go with us. To wait and tell him is the only right thing to do."

Judy looked at her in consternation. "Oh Susanne, we want to surprise him. For heaven's sake don't put a wet blanket on it. Don't you remember Aunt Alice told us José could be depended upon? So he'll take care of us. Don't act stubborn!" She turned to Marie, "It isn't very far up there, is it?"

For a moment Marie hesitated. "It will take two days, Señorita," she said slowly.

Even Judy was startled. "Two days!" she gasped. "My glory, I didn't think it was as far as that." Her heart sank. Susanne would now stay home for sure. But she went on doggedly. "I don't care how long it takes, I'm going! I shan't let a little thing like that—"

Susanne broke in hotly, "It's too far. And I don't care what Aunt Alice said about José, we shouldn't go without telling Colonel Thompson. It isn't fair to him or to Uncle Jim or Aunt Alice."

Judy's jaw set. She was going without telling anyone. "You can do as you please," she told Susanne. "I'm going! And if you telephone the Colonel or Aunt Alice, I'll never forgive you as long as I live."

Susanne was wondering how on earth she could stop her. She must! In spite of what Marie had said, they had been told by their uncle that it was unsafe to go up any of the rivers. Then, she wasn't so sure about José. It was this same supposedly trustworthy José who had fallen asleep, when he was guarding the idol at the monastery. Their aunt and the Colonel would be furious with them for going way up there. She knew there was no use in telephoning Colonel Thompson. Judy would be on her way long before he could arrive. The only thing that came to her was to refuse to go. No matter that Judy had stormed she would go by herself; Susanne was doubtful Judy would carry out her wild plan.

"Don't worry, I'm not telephoning," she said. "But you can't go by yourself. I am not going! And you wouldn't be so crazy as to go way up there with only José."

Judy's eyes were blazing. "Oh wouldn't I?" she said. "You just watch me. I'll show you whether I'll do it or not. I have the chance to get that idol, and I intend doing it." She turned to Marie. "Do you know where José is?"

"He is in the back courtyard, *Señorita*." Marie was all smiles. "I go after him. I get him for you."

"Okay. I'll run up and change my clothes. I'll be right down," Judy said, hurrying into the house.

Susanne followed her. She sat on the edge of her bed and watched Judy go to the closet bring out a pair of linen slacks and an old green sweater.

Judy never glanced at Susanne while she was getting into these things. Susanne sat there eying her despairingly, but not saying a word. It didn't seem possible Judy would go alone.

When Judy ran down stairs Susanne went over to the window. She saw Marie come from the back courtyard with the big, gangling José who did not have the quick, alert mind and movements of weazened old Pedro.

Marie was gesticulating and talking excitedly to José. He was nodding his head. Judy was running down the flower-bordered path to meet them. The three were now standing by the fountain talking. Then Susanne saw Marie start for the kitchen; José entered the back patio and Judy dashed into the house.

Judy raced up the stairs and burst into the room. "You've got to come with us, Susanne," she said breathlessly. "We're leaving in half an hour. José's getting the hammocks and other things. I'm going to the kitchen and help Marie with the food. Come on, honey," she smiled at her. "Hustle into your clothes. Be a good sport and come with me." She put her arm around Susanne and gave her a hug. "We'll have a swell time. I want you with me when I find the idol. Come on, old sour-face."

Susanne pushed Judy's arm away. "I'm not going, Judy. I told you I wasn't, and I meant it." She held her silver wrist watch so Judy might see the time. "Look, it's half past four. It's too late to start. Please wait and telephone Colonel Thompson. He'll take us tomorrow. Don't do this crazy thing. It isn't necessary, Judy."

Judy was beginning to realize it was insane, and might prove dangerous. But she was too stubborn to give in. "I'm not asking Colonel Thompson to help get back the idol," she told her. "I'm getting it back myself. You stay right here. I wouldn't let you go with me now if you'd beg on your hands and knees." She went over to her bureau, opened a drawer, took out her flash-light and hurried from the room.

CHAPTER X

UP LITTLE *El Negro*

In less than half an hour, José, Marie and Judy were on their way to the river, laden with provisions, hammocks, blankets, rope, machetes and other things necessary for the trip.

Judy was standing in the clumsy dugout canoe poking hammocks under a seat, when Susanne came racing down the forest trail. She was still wearing her green dress and with her fair hair and pink and white coloring she made Judy think of a lovely wood nymph.

She was calling, "Wait for me, Judy! I'm going with you. Wait for me!"

Judy's heart leaped at the sight of her. She had been praying Susanne would not let her go alone.

"Oh boy, I'm all out of breath!" Susanne panted. She rubbed her hand across her damp forehead and smiled sheepishly at Judy. "Glad to see me?"

Judy grinned and gave the hammocks another poke. "Of course not. You silly thing. Don't you know I hate you?"

"Sure I do," Susanne laughed. She threw

across a seat the old black sweater she had brought along and stepped into the dugout. "I hate you too. Don't get conceited and think I like you. The only reason I came is for the canoe trip." Her eyes lit on part of a hammock sticking out from under the seat. She hadn't one. José would have to return to the plantation and they'd lose valuable time. Ashamed and disturbed she told Judy.

Judy laughed and held up three fingers. "As always, I looked out for you, you poor little kid."

Their eyes met. Susanne said, "You knew I would come, didn't you?"

A lump rose in Judy's throat. Susanne was such a darling. She had fought against this trip, but in spite of it, would not let her go alone.

"You're the swellest girl I know," she said slowly. "The swellest, grandest girl in the whole world." She leaned down picked up a paddle and handed it to her. "You take the middle seat, Susanne. I'm paddling from the bow, José is steering. All right, José. Get in now. We're ready."

José shoved off the boat and got in.

"Good-bye, Marie!" Judy called. "We'll be seeing you tomorrow evening. If Colonel Thompson comes tell him not to worry. We'll be all right. And take good care of Rosetta."

Marie's face was wreathed in smiles. "*Adiós, Señoritas!* I tell the *Señor,* and I take care of Rosetta. You will find the idol; of that I am certain."

It was seven o'clock when they turned off *El Negro* onto a smaller river, a branch as swift and nearly as wide as the one they had been on.

The stream twisted and turned like a green snake between the deep forest. The moon rose and at times it would be directly in front of them and they seemed to travel on a sea of moving silver.

Susanne was very quiet. It worried Judy. She wondered if Susanne might be afraid. She smiled back at her and said with great enthusiasm, "Isn't this beautiful! I've never seen anything like it."

Susanne lifted her paddle and brought it through the water. "I'm not exactly crazy about it. This old river's too weird, too ghostly." She drew a deep breath. "José, how much longer are we paddling? Isn't it almost time to stop and make camp?"

José was steering the dugout around a bend in the river. "You are tired, *Señorita?*" he asked anxiously.

"No, I'm not tired," Susanne said quickly. "I only wondered, that's all."

"That is good." José's voice showed his relief.

"We camp after awhile, when we come to a cleared place. See, no place here."

That was true; heavy vines and creepers twisted themselves about the great trees like venomous snakes, making a barrier clear to the water's edge.

Again and again, Susanne held her flashlight so she might see the time on her wrist watch. Nine o'clock, then ten o'clock, and still no sign of José stopping to make camp.

Like Judy, every summer she had spent two months at a camp. She was an expert paddler and was not tired. Often she had gone on longer and harder trips than this. But this was far different. The river, the forest, the intense darkness and shimmering moonlight were all so ghostly, so uncanny, it was making her nervous. She was eager for a camp where their hammocks would be hung before a cheery, blazing fire.

Judy was not affected by the weirdness of the scene. She was too intent upon recovering the idol. She was thinking how surprised and happy Colonel Thompson would be. Her anger flamed at Phil. At last, he was being found out. There was no doubt in her mind but that he had taken the idol. What other reason could he possibly have to come way up here except to hide the idol? It was lucky for them that Ricardo's friend had seen him. This Indian, Ricardo and Marie must all share in the reward. Susanne's diamond ring naturally, would be given to Marie if it were proven that she had not stolen the jewelry.

On and on they went. It was nearly midnight when José said, "See that clearing to the right? We go there. A good place to camp that is."

Susanne began to paddle fast. "Let's get there soon as we can. I'm not tired, but my legs are cramped from all this sitting."

"I'm glad we're not camping in any dark woods," Judy said happily. "It's as bright as day in that big open space. And am I hungry! Oh boy, I'm hollow clear down to my toes. How about you, Susanne?"

"Hungry enough to eat a bear," Susanne laughed. Then added quickly, "But I hope there's none around. Are there any in this old woods, José?"

"No bears," José told her.

"Any other wild animals?" Susanne persisted. "Any fierce ones?"

José was heading the dugout toward the shore. "Pumas and wild hogs and tigers. You afraid? You must not be afraid, our fire will keep them away."

Susanne gave a nervous little laugh. "Not exactly afraid. But I'd rather see a wild animal in a zoo than out here."

"Paddle hard, *Señoritas!* Paddle hard!" José ordered. *"Bueno! Bueno!"*

With strong swift strokes, the girls were bringing their paddles through the water. There was the sound of the boat scraping the pebbly beach. Before José could climb over the seats and get out, Judy and Susanne were on the shore attempting to pull the boat in a little further.

"You smart. You know how," José chuckled, getting out as fast as his rheumatic legs would permit him. "You very smart."

Judy laughed. "Not smart, only hungry. We're dying for something to eat."

José dragged the heavy boat up on the tiny beach. The girls helped carry the provisions, hammocks, blankets and other things to the clearing. They watched as he hung their hammocks on the edge of the forest then helped him search for dry wood for their fire. Soon a bright blaze was burning and the three were eating their belated supper.

It was half past twelve by the time they finished their meal and were in their hammocks. In five minutes Susanne was sound asleep. But not Judy. She was too excited. José had told them that the cave was only a few miles away. In the morning they would have only two hours of paddling, then they would be there. Why had

Phil taken the idol, she wondered? Colonel Thompson had told her that Phil's father was very generous with him, so Phil couldn't possibly have taken it because he needed money. She lay there trying to figure it out, but finally gave it up.

At night, a tropical forest is anything but quiet. In the dense woods back of her, Judy could hear twigs cracking, a bush dog yowled off in the distance, then abruptly stopped his yapping. An owl hooted and there was the cry of birds flying low.

Ever so often she saw José get out of his hammock for more wood. He made grotesque shadows as he replenished the fire.

It was after two o'clock when at last she fell asleep. She was awakened by something; she didn't know what. She had a feeling that a strange person, or an animal was near her hammock. Her eyes were wide with fright as she slowly raised her head and looked around. The glow of the fire, José's and Susanne's hammocks were all she could see. "I'm so keyed up I'm imagining things," she said to herself as she lay down again. "I hope to goodness I don't imagine any more hair raising things like that."

She was almost asleep, when again, she had that uncanny feeling. Some one was standing near her. She knew now that there was no mistake about this. Cold perspiration broke out on her and she lay there scarcely breathing. José was snoring. There was no other sound, save the thumping of her heart. This time it required all the will power she possessed to open her eyes and see what it was.

A man was standing by the tree to which the foot of her hammock was hung!

She slid to the ground and went racing across the clearing calling frantically, "José! Oh José!"

"What's wrong, *Señorita!* What's wrong?" he asked in alarm.

Judy grabbed his arm. "A man's over by that tree!" Her voice was hysterical as she pointed to the half concealed figure. "See him? Oh there he goes into the woods!" Yelling loudly, José chased after him.

Susanne was sitting up in her hammock asking in a trembling voice, "Judy, what's happened? What's the matter?"

Judy said weakly, "Oh my glory, a man was standing by that tree staring at me. He scared me almost to death."

"Oh my heavens!" Susanne gasped.

In a few minutes José reappeared shoving a middle aged, tall, lanky Indian in front of him.

"He not hurt you," José laughed. "He Francisco. He work on Stanton's plantation. He drunk. He say he up river visiting his people; on way to plantation when he saw our fire and came over."

The big fellow was grinning good naturedly. "Me Francisco," he announced pointing to himself.

Phil had told the girls about him. Francisco had saved Phil's life and in spite of the Indian's weakness for drink, Phil was devoted to him.

Susanne was gazing at the man with interest. Judy was not the least interested in him, she was far too angry. "You're a fine one," she said wrathfully. "Don't you know any better than to stare at a person when she's sleeping! You almost frightened the life out of me. Don't you ever do such a—" She stopped, for through her mind was racing the question, "Could he have helped Phil hide the idol?" She went on in a different tone, "Was Phil up river with you, Francisco?"

Francisco nodded. "Si, Señorita, he was with me. He gone now."

"Yes I know." She went over close to him and asked smiling, "Francisco, would you like to make a lot of money?"

"Oh, Señorita, si, si." Francisco's black eyes were sparkling. "I like it much."

"All right. You tell us where the idol is. If

you do you'll not only get the reward, but Miss Susanne and I will give you something beside. You know where the thief hid the idol, don't you, Francisco?"

"Si, I know where the idol is," Francisco admitted readily.

He knew! Francisco knew! Judy was so happy she felt like hugging the old, smiling Indian. She asked breathlessly, "Where is it, Francisco?"

The Indian's face became stolid. "I not tell."

José was chuckling. He poked Francisco in the ribs and said, "Oh caramba, you don't know. You drunk. You bragging."

Francisco reeled a bit, but managed to stand very erect. He said with much dignity, "Francisco does not lie. When he say he know where idol is, Francisco knows."

"Does Phil know too?" Susanne asked in her gentle voice.

Francisco nodded vigorously, "Si, Señorita, Phil know. Phil know, Francisco know and—" he considered for a moment, then went on, "and other people know."

The girls were sure he was telling the truth; José was skeptical but, he too, coaxed Francisco to tell; he too threatened the stubborn old fellow and pleaded with him.

Judy said, "Think Francisco, what you could do with all that money! You'd have more than any Indian on the place. You'd be rich. You don't want any one else to get the reward, do you?"

Francisco rubbed a very dirty hand across his mouth and eyed her sullenly.

When he had left and they were once more in their hammocks it was hard for Judy to keep back the tears. She felt sure that their trip up here would amount to nothing. Francisco never asked why they had come up river. But she was certain the drunken but foxy old fellow had a suspicion. If the idol were in the cave, it wouldn't be there when they arrived. Why did he have to see their fire and come over here? She wished they had watched which way he went. But there was no doubt in her mind but what he had turned the dugout around and had started back up river. The only thing for them to do was to go to the cave, for even though it was hopeless, they would keep on and finish what they had set out to do.

The next morning she awoke at five-thirty. There was sunshine and dew and fragrance. On a tree over Susanne's head were three gorgeous lavender-pink orchids.

For a few moments she sensed only the beauty

of the place. Then she remembered what had happened: Francisco had frightened her; they had found out that he, Phil and others knew where the thief or thieves had taken the idol. She was certain Phil was involved, otherwise Francisco would have talked in order to get the reward.

After a hurried breakfast, they reloaded the dugout and continued their journey up river.

"Do you know what I hope?" Judy brought her paddle savagely through the water. "I hope that when they catch Phil, Francisco and the rest of that gang, they'll put them in jail for twenty years! They deserve that and more too."

José was steering the boat around a bend in the river. "I do not believe Phil stole the idol," he said calmly.

Judy flared. "Don't talk so idiotically, José. Why did he come up here? Why wouldn't he tell us the reason?"

José too, had wondered about that. He shrugged his shoulders. "I do not know, Señorita. José does not know."

Judy said, "Of course you don't. And when we get up there, we'll find the idol has been taken away."

José did not say any more. Susanne was as angry at Phil as Judy and was as disturbed, but showing it would not help matters.

"Come on, Judy, let's sing. I'm not going to allow Phil and his old gang to spoil my ride up this beautiful river. Look, there's a monkey in that tree! See him? And see those lovely pink flowers." She began to sing, and at last, Judy joined in.

In less than two hours they were dragging the dugout up on a long beach on which were a number of canoes. José told them that the dugouts belonged to Indians who lived in villages deep in the jungle.

"Is it one of these places Francisco comes from?" Judy wanted to know.

"Si, and Ricardo, too. Ricardo's tribe lives far far in there." José was getting his machete out of the boat. He slipped the heavy knife into a sheath hanging from his leather belt.

"So Ricardo lives up here!" Judy flared. "What a liar Marie is. She told us that Ricardo couldn't come up here for he didn't know this part of the country. Can't that girl be honest with us at all?"

José looked astonished. "She say that? *Si,* Marie she lie. She know Ricardo live up this Little *El Negro.*" He shrugged his shoulders. "Why she say that I don't know." He gave the girls their flashlights and they started up the trail.

"Phil must have been crazy to hide the idol

along this trail," Judy said as they trudged along. "Indians must come down here every day."

"Si, they come down river to fish," José chuckled. "Indians not like caves, they stay out. Indians think bad spirits live in caves. But old José knows better."

Susanne gave a nervous little laugh. "If I hear anything more about spirits or ghosts, I'll turn up my toes and die. You'll have to go in first, José, and if you don't yell we'll know it's all right."

His black eyes were twinkling. "I go first, Señorita. Do not worry. I not let bad spirit eat you up."

In half an hour they were almost at their destination and the trail now was so narrow they were having a difficult time to get through. Susanne who was in the rear was working to free her dress from a long vine covered with briars, when someone reached out of the jungle, grabbed her arms and began dragging her into the forest.

She let out one scream after another. Judy turned, too petrified to move. Shouting, José ran to Susanne's rescue.

To his amazement he found it was Francisco who was dragging Susanne into the woods. It wasn't difficult to free the girl and to knock the drunken fellow to the ground. Leaning down and shaking him José asked why he had done such a dastardly thing.

Francisco mumbled that he didn't want the Señoritas to go to the cave. Bad place that was and the idol was not there.

Susanne stood looking down at him and rubbing her right arm. "Don't hit him again," she pleaded. "He's too drunk to know what he's doing. Oh please don't hit him."

José nodded. "Si, he drunk. He would not hurt you, only scare you. I not hit him. But I get him out of here."

He yanked the Indian to his feet, pushed him out to the trail. "You go home," he roared. "You get in your dugout and go back to the plantation. Get out now! Go on!" he ordered pushing him along.

Francisco almost fell when José let go of him. Then bracing himself, he went staggering down toward the river.

As they went along it was all Susanne could do to keep back the tears, but she protested she was all right and would not even permit them to look at her bruised arms.

The cave was easy to locate, for it was in an enormous boulder close to the trail. It was smaller than the chapel in the monastery, so it did not take long to go over every inch of it. The floor was covered with piles of dried leaves blown in from outside and there were many bones of small animals. There was nothing else. Francisco was right. The jade idol was not there.

Judy was cruelly disappointed. She had been hoping against hope that she might be wrong, that Francisco might have thought the idol so safe he would not disturb it. But drunk as he was he had taken it away. He had probably hid it in the jungle and she felt sure that he was too drunk to ever recall where he had hid it. All she wanted to do now was to get home as fast as they could.

On their way down to the river they did not see anything of Francisco. There were many dugouts along the bank, but José couldn't tell if any belonged to Francisco so they did not know whether he had started for home or not.

Paddling down stream Judy began thinking of Colonel Thompson and what he was going to say to them for leaving the plantation and coming way up here. "I dread seeing him," she said to Susanne. "He's going to be furious with us."

"He'll give us blue blazes," Susanne said gloomily as she brought her paddle swiftly through the water. "And what Aunt Alice will

say won't sound so pleasant either. Well, anyway, we know Phil did take the idol."

"A lot of good that will do us," Judy said,
"when we don't know where it is."

They paddled with the current, and made the
homeward journey in rapid time. It was only a
little after dark when they arrived at the ford, and
dead tired, the girls went up the forest trail to
the house.

Marie heard them enter the patio and came
racing down stairs. "Señoritas, did you find the
idol?" she called. "Did you find the idol?"

Judy dropped on a chair and let the empty
saddlebag fall to the ground.

"No, we didn't find it, Marie," she said wearily.
"How is Rosetta? Has Colonel Thompson been
here?"

CHAPTER XI

THE COLONEL QUESTIONS MARIE

MARIE DID not answer Judy's questions. She went on talking about how sorry she was that the idol was not in the cave. She was far too sympathetic to sound genuine and Judy eyed her suspiciously. But Judy had too many things on her mind to worry about Marie.

"Why don't you answer me, Marie! How is Rosetta? And has Colonel Thompson telephoned or been here?"

Marie told her that the Colonel had been there. He wanted them to call him as soon as they got in. Their aunt too, wanted them to telephone. Rosetta was not feeling so well.

Judy was looking so unhappy and miserable, Susanne felt sorry for her. It was bad enough not to find the idol and now Judy would be given the very old dickens for going up river.

"You sit still," she said to her. "I'll run in and do the telephoning. I'll be out in a jiffy."

She was racing into the house when Judy caught up with her. Judy hadn't dreamed that she would have to go through this ordeal the minute she got home. She thought the Colonel would come in the morning when she would feel rested and more able to take the scolding she knew awaited her. It was then too, she had planned to telephone her Aunt Alice.

She said, "I got you into this Susanne, and I'm the one who will take the blame. You're not doing any telephoning."

She called her aunt first who was so relieved to hear Judy's voice and to learn that the girls were home safe and sound, that she scolded very little.

It was a different story when she telephoned Colonel Thompson. He was astonished at Judy for being so gullible as to start out on only Marie's fantastic tale.

Judy protested that it wasn't a fantastic tale. Phil had taken the idol up river, an Indian had seen him at the cave and had told Ricardo.

The Colonel said it sounded mighty strange to him. If true, Ricardo would have been so eager to get the reward that he would have gone himself. Marie's explanation didn't make sense. He had heard their Uncle Jim tell them that it was unsafe for them to go up any of the rivers and stay all night. In spite of this they had done it and without permission or telling anyone. He said much more. When he finished, Judy slowly hung up the receiver. "Whew," she gasped. "I sure got all that was coming to me, and then some! Susanne, did you hear everything he said?"

Susanne had been sharing the telephone with Judy. "Did I hear it? If he had said anything more I'd have screamed," she said furiously, "What right had he to talk to you like that. Who does he think he is, anyway? He hasn't charge of us."

"Of course he hasn't!" Judy hadn't thought of that. And now she was beginning to feel not only sorry for herself, but very much abused. It was true they had gone up river without telling anyone, or asking permission, but nothing serious had happened. She certainly hadn't anything to do with Rosetta being shot, or the stealing of the idol. If Phil did steal it it wasn't her fault. This was Phil's second home and Colonel Thompson had told them several times that their uncle had allowed Phil to take the key to the chapel when a treasure had been brought there for safe keeping.

She said hotly, "Of course he hasn't charge of us! He makes me sick. Every blessed thing that's happened has been his fault. If he hadn't brought that old jade idol to the monastery we wouldn't be in this mess. Come on, let's find out how Rosetta is, then take a bath and go to bed."

Rosetta did have a fever, but too slight to worry about. So it was not Rosetta who was on Judy's mind as she lay awake that night. Judy was thinking about Phil, Francisco and others, trying to figure things out.

Unless Phil had unintentionally left the chapel door unlocked, it was he who stole the idol. It could not be anyone else. But who stole Susanne's jewelry, and why were hers the only ones taken? Who was it who had climbed up to their room and stolen the key?

In spite of what she had said to the Colonel, she realized that it was mighty strange Ricardo and Marie had not gone after the idol themselves. It had been in the cave. Judy felt sure of that. So why did Ricardo and Marie want Susanne and her to go? The reward was more than Marie and Ricardo could earn in years. This didn't make sense. Why hadn't Francisco returned it and claimed the reward? There was some reason they were not doing it. It was beyond her; she couldn't make it out. Judy dreaded the morning, when she would face a scolding not only from Pedro, but from Colonel Thompson as well. That wasn't a happy thing to look forward to. She didn't know how she could stand another session with him.

She was so upset she was still awake at two o'clock. She lifted up the mosquito netting canopy, slid out of bed, took a box of chocolates from the stand and went over to a chair by the window.

She was sitting there munching candy and looking out on the moonlit patio when she saw a man come out of the house. It was Pedro! He was carrying two things covered with a white cloth. One was large and flat, the other small like a bowl. He was walking fast and kept glancing around as though he did not want anyone to see him.

When he had disappeared through the archway Judy gasped, "What under heavens is Pedro doing here this time of night? And what is he taking away? Could he be the one who is doing the stealing?" she wondered. That was a crazy thought. Pedro would be the last one to suspect. But why didn't he want anyone to see him? Suddenly, she became afraid. She set down the box of candy and scurried across the room to her bed.

In the morning she hurried down stairs before Susanne to see if she could discover what was missing. It did not take her long to see that the large, heavily embossed silver tray always on the dining room side board was not there.   Also gone was a tall, silver goblet, one of four used for icewater.

Susanne appeared in the doorway.   She was wearing very gay shorts and looking as fresh as a rose.   "The top of the morning to you!   Thought I'd be stiff from sitting so long in that old dugout. But darling, look at me!"   She danced around the table, then grabbed Judy.   "Come on, make your feet fly.   Let's have a swing before breakfast."

Judy pushed her away.   "We have something more important to think of than dancing.   What do you suppose has happened now?"

Startled at Judy's grave manner, Susanne asked weakly, "What?   Oh Lordy, has anything else terrible happened?"

Judy nodded.   "Last night Pedro stole Aunt Alice's large silver tray and one of her silver goblets."

She told her what she had seen.   Susanne stood with her hands on her hips and stared at Judy. "Are you crazy?   Have you lost your senses? What if Pedro did take those things.   That's nothing.   You know well enough that Indians often work at night.   He probably has them in the back courtyard cleaning them."

"Indians do work in the fields when it's moonlight," Judy said.   "But house servants work only in the daytime. Another thing, Pedro didn't go to the back courtyard. He went out the archway to the trail."

Susanne pleaded with Judy not to say anything to him. "Don't accuse him," she begged. "It would break his heart if he knew you thought he was a thief. If he doesn't return them you tell Aunt Alice when she comes home. It's up to her to do something about it. Don't tell a soul, Judy. We're in enough messes right now. Keep out of this, please!"

Judy's face was grave as finally she promised and they went out of the room to their breakfast in the patio.

All morning there was no sign of Pedro. Judy inquired, but the cook, Marie or José knew nothing about him.

Judy was about to call, "Good morning!" as the Colonel rode through the archway but his face was so grim she stood there holding her basket of flowers and eyed him antagonistically. She had had her scolding. Enough was enough. If he started in on her again she would tell him a few things.

Susanne called a greeting. The Colonel nodded, got off his horse, threw the reins across a bush and came clanking across the courtyard.

He announced that he had come over to ques-

"All right. Now who told Ricardo?"

Marie again glanced pleadingly at Judy. "Oh Señor, I do not know. I—I tell you I do not know."

The Colonel was eyeing her suspiciously. "Very well. We'll have Ricardo come here. I intend finding out who the man was that saw Phil up at that cave. Get Ricardo, Marie."

Marie's black eyes were wide with fright. "No, no, do not ask Ricardo! Please, Señor. Do not make me bring him here. Please!"

The Colonel leaned forward. "Why, Marie? Why not? You answer me!" he demanded sharply.

Marie stood there looking at him with tear filled eyes, saying not a word.

"Because you lied! No one saw Master Phil up at that cave. Isn't that the truth?" he thundered.

Marie shook her head. "No, Señor. I did not lie," she muttered in a low voice. "I did not lie. Some one did see him."

"You're lying, Marie! You sent the girls up there on a miserable lie. If you were telling the truth you'd bring Ricardo. Why you had the girls go up there I don't know, but I intend to find out! Ricardo is coming here." He banged his fist on the arm of his chair. "Hear me? If you won't go after him, I'll send some one else."

Marie buried her face in her hands and began to sob. "I say Ricardo told me a man saw Master Phil up river. Ricardo told me, Señor. Ricardo gone home. He not here."

Judy's heart ached for the girl. She leaned down and rearranged the pink rose in Marie's black hair. "Don't cry," she whispered. "It's all right, Marie. I believe you and I'm sure Miss Susanne does too." She pleaded with the Colonel not to question Marie any longer. "I believe she's telling the truth. You have her terribly frightened. Just see how she's crying. Please, let her go," she begged.

The Colonel's face was livid with fury. "I saw Ricardo picking coffee when I came down from the camp. So you see she lied about him. You should have brains enough to realize that if Marie and Ricardo thought the idol was up in the cave they would have hustled up there themselves. They sent you on a fool's errand. And now you're asking me to stop questioning Marie. I'm astonished at you, Judy."

"All right, Marie. Go on. Get out of here!" he told her. "You beat it up to Rosetta's room and see if you can behave yourself for a little while. But I'm not letting you get away with this. I'm finding out what you and Ricardo were up to."

As they watched her scurry up the path and into the house, Susanne said slowly, "Well if she isn't something! She's as slick as they make them. Anyone who was smart enough to make us go on that crazy trip up river would be capable of stealing the idol. If she didn't take it, I'll bet she was the brains of the Indian or Indians who did."

Colonel Thompson agreed with Susanne. He said he had thought of stopping and questioning Ricardo, but had changed his mind. Ricardo would only lie. He would get to the bottom of this by some other method.

The Colonel had come over to question the Indian girl for another reason, too. He had brought very bad news. He waited until the girls had stopped talking about Marie and had calmed down a bit. Judy was refilling his tall glass with lemonade, when he asked quietly, "Have you girls heard that Phil has disappeared?"

Judy nearly dropped the large silver pitcher. "Phil has disappeared? They—they can't find him?"

The Colonel nodded. "Yes. No one has seen him since night before last."

Susanne was not alarmed. She reached over to the cookies on a stand and said calmly, "What on earth is there to worry about? He's gone up river for a couple of days, just as he's done before."

"He's not up river, Susanne," the Colonel said gravely. "We wouldn't be so worried, but not one dugout is missing."

Susanne's blue eyes tore open. "Oh—how about his horse? Is Major gone?"

"Major and every one of the horses are here. All yesterday and last night they've been searching for him. Naturally, his father is frantic. Judy, don't look so frightened. They'll find him. I'm sure of that."

With shaking hands Judy set the pitcher on the table. "Yes, but you don't know. They've been searching for a day and night and they haven't found him yet."

Ice tinkled in the Colonel's tall glass as he stirred his lemonade. "That's right. But I'm certain he'll be found, Judy, for he can't be far away." He tried to make his voice sound convincing. "It would be foolish to say we are not worried. Anyone would be. But what's happened isn't necessarily serious. Phil didn't go in a dugout, or ride his horse, so you see he is somewhere near by."

Suddenly Judy thought of something terrifying; her knees became so weak she sank on a chair. "Do—do you think he might have done something to himself because I accused him of stealing the idol?" she asked in a low, frightened voice.

Susanne rushed over to her. "Don't you ever say such a thing again!" She turned to Colonel Thompson. "Scold her, please. Make her get that crazy notion out of her head. Don't let her say such a thing."

Like a physician talking to an irrational patient, the Colonel leaned forward and said calmly, "I'm surprised at you, Judy. A sensible girl talking like that. You are in no way connected with his disappearance. What they think has happened, is that he went off on a hike and has fallen and hurt himself. Accidents such as that occur very often. As I said before, he can't be very far away. The Indians know every foot of this mountain. They are searching and will find him."

Judy pulled out her handkerchief and mopped her eyes. "I never knew so many terrible things to happen, and one right after another. If that darned old jade idol isn't a jinx I'll miss my guess!" She wanted to add, "And it's all your fault for finding the old thing." But she did not say it, she only glared at the Colonel and blew her nose.

Marie appeared on the balcony. "Rosetta is much worse!" she called. "Rosetta is much worse!"

They found her temperature very high. But the Colonel thought it only a flare up and was sure by morning it would be normal. Before riding off he said there was no need to worry about Phil either. "I'll keep you posted," he said. "And I'm sure you will have good news."

CHAPTER XII

WHAT JUDY OVERHEARD

I⊤ was a heartbreaking evening and night, for there was no good report about Phil, and Rosetta had become a very sick woman.

By three o'clock in the morning Judy and Susanne were so worn out and exhausted Marie begged the girls to lie down. Susanne went to her room, and Judy in order to be near Rosetta went out on the balcony and threw herself down on a couch.

Several hours later Judy was awakened by a low whistle. Marie ran out of the room and leaning over the balustrade called down softly, "Ricardo, I shall be there in a little minute. I am happy you have come."

She could hear the girl running down stairs, then a man's voice. It was evident that they had something important to talk about and something they wished to keep secret, for Marie kept warning, "Not so loud."

Judy was too indifferent and too well bred to attempt to listen to the conversation, but the word idol came to her. Like a flash she slid off the cot and stood there listening.

She had studied Spanish for a year and understood it quite well. Marie was now talking in such a low tone that only occasionally could she catch a word.

She heard, "idol . . . under the strong room. . . ." Soft laughter . . . then, "up river . . . Master Phil . . . thief . . . Señor Thompson. . . . I know how to get down there. . . ."

"You know, Marie!" Ricardo's voice was incredulous.

Marie forgetting caution herself exclaimed happily and loudly, "Si, si, I know. Out of her head Rosetta is. She talked about the baptistry. It moves, Ricardo. That is another way to get down under the monastery. What do we care now that we could not find the secret door. We know the baptistry moves," she laughed.

Judy could hear Ricardo laugh and pat Marie's bare arms.

"You are a saint. A beautiful saint. When it is dark tonight . . ." Ricardo's voice was too low to hear.

Then came Marie's voice also low and indistinct.

Again Ricardo laughed. "And then what?

We go to the big city of Mexico. And come back? No, Marie, *mia*. We shall spend much money and be gay and happy, for we shall be rich."

"*Bueno! Bueno!*" Marie laughed and clapped her hands. "What time shall I meet you tonight, Ricardo?"

"You come to the monastery when the moon is up. That will be all right, Marie?"

"Oh yes, Ricardo. I shall be there surely."

"At nine o'clock I shall see you there. *Adiós*, Marie, *mia*," Ricardo said softly.

A few minutes later Marie tiptoed out on the balcony. Judy lay with her eyes closed, the girl sure Judy was sound asleep, went humming into Rosetta's room.

Judy's anger flared at her. It was all she could do not to go in there and drive her from the house. But her better judgment told her that for the present, it was wiser to keep still.

So it was absolutely true Phil had stolen the idol and had taken it up river, but why were Marie and Ricardo going to the monastery tonight to steal it? One thing was sure, the idol was in a secret room underneath the monastery. If Phil had taken it up river, for some reason he had brought it back and hid it there.

If she could help it Phil never would lay eyes

on it again. As for Marie and Ricardo, they would have all their pains for nothing. Right now she and Susanne were going to the monastery and try to locate that room.

She glanced at her wrist watch. It was five o'clock. Often they had gone riding as early as this, so Marie would think nothing strange of it.

For a few minutes she lay there planning, then slid out of bed and went into Rosetta's room.

"How is she this morning, Marie?" she tried to make her voice sound as natural as possible.

Marie stopped fanning the sick woman, and smiling, rose to her feet.

"Better, Señorita. She is sleeping now. And you, did you sleep well?"

Judy ignored the question. She put her hand on Rosetta's forehead. "Her fever isn't so high. That's fine. I'll give her her medicine, then Miss Susanne and I are going for a ride. Will probably be back around seven o'clock."

Susanne was anything but pleased to be awakened. She opened one eye and glared at Judy. "Don't bother me. Let me alone, Judy. I want to sleep."

Judy leaned down and in a voice tense with excitement whispered, "Listen, we're going for a ride. Have found out something about the idol."

The word idol made Susanne sit up in a hurry. "Has it been found? Oh Judy, has it?" she asked eagerly.

Judy placed her fingers on her lips and glanced toward Rosetta's room. "No it hasn't," she whispered. "Mustn't talk now. But I think I know where it is. We're going to look for it. Get dressed, Susanne. Scram!"

Thrilled and excited, Susanne slid out of bed. "It'll not take me long," she said breathlessly. "I'll be ready in a jiffy."

All the time she was getting her riding outfit it was all she could do to keep from asking questions. But she realized from Judy's actions that whatever had happened, Judy was trying to keep it from Marie, so she must wait until they were away from the house.

When Judy got their flashlights, slipped hers into a pocket of her jodhpurs and handed the other to Susanne, her cousin gasped, "Good heavens, are we going into another cave? I hate caves, Judy!"

Judy shook her head and again touched her lips with her fingers. "Don't say another word until we get out of here," she whispered.

Not until they were on their way to the corral did Judy tell Susanne what she was planning to do.

Susanne stopped and looked at her aghast. "Is this what you got me up for! Have you lost your mind. My glory, Judy, didn't we go on a wild goose chase up to that cave? We know Marie lied. No Indian had seen Phil up there. Now you come with this crazy story. Phil had the idol up river but has brought it back to a secret room under the monastery. If that doesn't sound fishy!"

"It doesn't sound fishy," Judy protested. "We know for sure Phil did go up river. Anyway, where ever he had the idol he did bring it back to this room. Ricardo was terribly excited this morning. So was Marie. They didn't know I was listening, so their talk wasn't for my benefit. What burns me up is that Marie planned this thing. She sure is a bad one. Well, we'll spoil their little party. They'll be sick when they discover the idol is gone. And they'll be sicker yet when I tell what I overheard."

Susanne was convinced Judy knew what she was talking about. What worried her now was whether they could make the baptistry move. As they walked along they discussed it and decided if they found it impossible, they would have to go back for Pedro and see if he could help. And when they found the idol, it wasn't getting away from them again; it was to be locked up in Judy's trunk and they'd have Pedro or José guarding it when they were out of the room.

When they stopped at a little building for their bridles, Judy picked up a saddlebag and a piece of burlap. "Meant to bring a towel, but forgot it," she said, slipping the saddlebag across her arm. Her eyes were grave as she added, "I'm not exactly afraid to touch the idol. But Susanne, if there is anything to that curse, I'm not doing anything more to bring it upon me."

Susanne changed her bridle to her other hand. "You're not touching it again. Not even when it is wrapped in that burlap. You've done enough. Now it's my turn. I'll put the idol in the saddle-bag." A frightened look had come in Judy's eyes, the same Susanne had seen many times before. She said with a little laugh, "Here we stand talking about being scared of a piece of stone. We certainly are two little ninnies. Come on, Judy, let's be going."

They caught and bridled their animals, mounted bareback and with Judy in the lead, went galloping down the trail to the monastery.

Judy wished with all her heart they were going for a long, care-free ride, instead of on the mission for which they were headed. In a few minutes they would probably be in an old damp room under a haunted monastery. Not a very cheerful thing to look forward to. She wondered how Susanne was feeling by this time. She pulled her horse to a canter and glanced back at her cousin. As she expected, Susanne was looking anything but happy.

"Hi there, do you want to see yourself?" she called. She drew down the corners of her mouth and made her eyes large and frightened looking.

Susanne grinned. "You're not hurting my feelings. That's exactly the way I feel. I get panicky every time I go into a cave or an old dark, mouldy smelling cellar. I was locked in a cellar once and never got over the fright. Why couldn't that old idol be hidden up in a tree, or some sunshiny, cheerful place? You won't mind going down in there, will you? Oh of course, you won't."

Judy colored. "I'm not one bit afraid," she lied valiantly. "Not one tiny bit."

Susanne eyed her accusingly, "Like fun you're not. You're nearly scared out of your wits right now." She laughed a little. "Poor me, I'm so frightened I'm weak in the pit of my stomach."

Judy too felt nervous, but she wasn't letting on. "There's nothing to be afraid of. We have our flashlights, so we'll not be in the dark. Oh Susanne I can hardly wait to get to that room. Come on, let's hurry."

They were quiet the rest of the way. Their silence held when they rode into the courtyard, tied their horses to the stone balustrade, went up the moss-covered steps and down the cloister to the old chapel.

It was too early for shafts of sunlight to filter in through the narrow, barred windows, so the girls entered a chapel filled with ghostly shadows.

Susanne glanced fearfully around and got closer to Judy. "Whew, I feel as if somebody's going to jump out at me! This sure is a spooky place."

Judy was going across the room to the baptismal font. "Don't talk like that," she scolded. "You'll get me jittery too. You can see there's no one in this room. There's no place for anyone to hide."

A few seconds later they were standing before the old stone baptistry examining it and trying to determine how it worked.

"I'm going to try this," Judy said. She gripped the edge of the heavy basin and attempted to pull it forward. It didn't budge.

"I'll bet it turns, Judy," Susanne said. "That's what Marie told Ricardo, wasn't it?"

"No, Marie just said that it moves. But I believe that's the way you do it. Anyhow, there's no harm in trying."

They attempted to turn it first in one direction, then in another, but with no success.

Judy rubbed her perspiring hands on her riding breeches.

"Maybe it tilts. Let's try that and see what happens. Grab hold, Susanne."

They were using very little force, when Judy gasped, "It's moving! It's moving! It's going back into the inset."

Susanne whispered excitedly, "Look out for the hole. Be careful. Don't fall in."

"No, I'll be careful," Judy told her as they tilted the heavy stone font way back into the alcove. "Oh Susanne, we have found the entrance. Isn't it wonderful to know we've found it. Let's push it a couple times as hard as we can so it will be sure to stay."

She was thinking what if the baptistry should come back into place while they were down below. She did not mention her fears to Susanne, but she made quite certain the baptistry was tilted so far into the inset that it could not move forward.

Susanne was leaning down peering into the darkness. "My soul, Judy, it's as black as Egypt! I never saw a place as dark as this."

Neither had Judy seen any place as black as the hole into which they were looking. It was going to take every bit of courage she could muster to go down in there.

She made herself say cheerfully, "Oh, it isn't so bad, Susanne. Any hole would be dark." She pulled her flashlight from her pocket. "Let's take a look before we go down and see what's in there."

Their lights revealed a long pair of stairs. But whether a room or tunnel was at the bottom it was impossible to make out.

Judy picked up the saddlebag.

"Come on, honey, I'm going now."

Susanne drew a long breath.

"Okay Judy, I'll be close behind you."

CHAPTER XIII

UNDER THE MONASTERY

THE STEPS were very steep and the stairs so long it seemed to the girls that they would never reach the bottom. At last they were down and were in what first appeared to be a tunnel.

But they had walked only a short distance, when Judy whispered in an awe-struck voice, "Good heavens, Susanne, this isn't a tunnel. It's a catacomb!"

"A catacomb!" Susanne's voice was almost a shriek. "It couldn't be, Judy. Oh Judy, it couldn't be that!"

Judy tried to keep her voice from trembling. "It is. Can't you see these burial places cut out of the rock?"

Susanne threw her flashlight along the wall. "Oh yes, I see them." Terrified, she clutched Judy's arm. "Let's get out of here. I can't go any further. There must be hundreds of dead people buried down here. Come on, Judy, let's go back."

Judy stood still. Could this be a burial place, or was it only to show what the catacombs in

Rome were like? But it didn't make any difference. They had to go on even though the tunnel
was lined with graves.

"I'm not going back," she said slowly. "Dead
people can't hurt us."

Susanne begged her not to go. "I don't care
if they can't. Who wants to go prowling around
where they are! And listen to that water dripping. Please, please Judy, let's go home."

Judy knew it would be useless to try to con-
vince Susanne that there were no dead people
down here. The only thing to do was to go on.
Susanne would not return alone. She would be
as afraid to do that as to stay.

She broke away from her saying, "You do as
you please. I told you I'm going on and I am."

Susanne was almost crying as she started after
her. "You're cruel, Judy," she kept saying.
"You're cruel."

"Don't step on my heels," Judy said nervously.
"Keep back a little. And be careful, for the floor
is slippery."

For a few minutes they went on in silence.
Judy flashed her light into a room which was
about the size of a large closet. "Here's a little
sacrament chapel. It's like one Mother and I
saw in Rome. It's lovely, isn't it?"

Susanne gave one glance. She was not interested in sacrament chapels, but only in getting out of this dungeon-like place. "Don't stop, Judy. The idol isn't there. This old tunnel may wind and wind. And if others lead off of this we can get lost as easy as scat. Look down the passageway. It's darker than pitch."

"It isn't dark where we're walking," Judy told her. "Our flashlights are making a good light."

A voice called out something in Spanish. It was so low and hollow it sounded like the voice of a ghost.

The girls stopped.

All they could now hear was the drip, drip of water and the beating of their hearts.

Louder now, again the person called.

The girls could not understand what he was saying, but both knew it was Phil.

Judy was all agog. She grabbed Susanne's arm. "Keep still!" she whispered. "We want to catch him red handed with the idol. Oh Susanne, we're catching him! See that light? That's where he is. Oh boy, we're catching him!"

Susanne was as excited as Judy. A faint glow was coming from the side of the gallery quite a distance from where they were. "Do you suppose that old drunken Francisco is with him?" she asked fearfully.

Judy told her that she didn't believe Francisco had come down from up river, but he might be there. "Don't talk any more," she whispered. "We don't want Phil to hear us."

They went on scarcely breathing, their eyes fixed on the faint gleam.

In spite of Phil's guilt, Susanne felt sorry that such a swell fellow as Phil had got himself into such a terrible mess. Why he had done it she couldn't figure out. What was back of this? she wondered. Susanne didn't believe he had stolen the idol for the money he could get out of it. There was some other reason. She thought of his father and how dreadfully he would feel the disgrace. Would they send Phil to prison? Perhaps they couldn't do anything else, but allow the law to take its course. The thrill over catching him was gone. She was too heart sick, too full of pity for Phil and his father.

There was no compassion in Judy's heart. She was so angry with him she rejoiced that she was going to catch him and see that he got what he deserved.

They turned out their flashlights so Phil would not know they were coming. Susanne tripped over a loose stone. After that they walked even more slowly than before.

They kept touching the walls and several times

came to open spaces which they thought might be other galleries. When they were almost there Susanne whispered. "I'm frightened, Judy. I'm terribly frightened."

Judy took a firmer grip of Susanne's hand.

"It doesn't make any difference," she said. "We're going on just the same."

Four steps more, and what they saw was so unexpected, so terrifying, they stood transfixed.

CHAPTER XIV

THEIR STARTLING DISCOVERY

THEY WERE at the entrance of a deep, shadowy cavern, dimly lighted by pine torches at the entrance and along the sides. Peering between the long stalactites which hung from the ceiling in grotesque masses, they could see a little fire burning at the end of the room, and over in the corner, what appeared to be an enormous, hideous idol.

Susanne was almost hysterical. "I can't go in, Judy," she whispered. Look at those long things hanging from the ceiling. They look like long arms ready to grab us. And see that idol! Please, please, let's go home."

Someone was moving down there in the semi-darkness. Judy leaned forward, her eyes focused on the spectral figure. For only a moment did she catch a glimpse of him before he disappeared behind a high, rocky formation.

"Keep quiet," she whispered. "Did you see that man? Keep still!"

Immediately, the man reappeared. For a few

minutes he was on his haunches busily engaged with something. Then picking up a long object, again he disappeared behind the screen-like rock.

Susanne tried to pull Judy away. "We'd be crazy to go in there! I tell you Judy, we'd be crazy. That fellow might kill us, Judy. You know he might."

Judy realized it was true, they might be killed. Who that man was she didn't know. But certainly he wasn't Francisco. Francisco was much taller and larger in every way.

She looked fearfully at the rock behind which the man had disappeared. For an instant she was panicky. It was all she could do not to run.

Somehow, she pulled herself together. She said, "I'm going in. You wait for me here." From now on she couldn't be responsible for this cousin of hers. She said again, "You wait right here, Susanne. I'll be all right."

She started into the cavern.

Susanne faltered, then white-faced, breathless, caught up with her. "I'm going with you," she said.

"Okay," Judy whispered. "But don't turn on your flashlight. I don't want Phil or that person to learn we're here until we catch them."

Very quietly they went down the long room.

To their relief what they thought was an idol was only a large, weird shaped boulder. Judy was too intent upon finding Phil and the War God to give it more than a passing glance. Neither one was in this room and she turned toward the place in which the man had disappeared.

For a brief moment her heart almost stopped beating. Could she make herself go back there? Could she? But for only a moment did she hesitate, then taking Susanne's hand, went over to the rock.

She decided to use caution and not go in until they had found out what was going on in there. Standing in the shadow, they peered around the screen-like rock.

Susanne gave a gasp of horror. Judy clapped her hand over Susanne's mouth. "Keep quiet," she whispered frantically. "For heaven's sake, keep quiet!"

Again they looked. The rock proved to be one side of a grotto. In contrast to the deep shadows there was a cascade of dripstones which formed the rear wall and which sparkled and glittered like a frozen Niagara.

A crude table stood before this dazzling background, and on it was the jade idol. The jade idol sitting very erect, his yellow eyes more terrifying than ever.* Pedro was standing by the table polishing an old gun.

Phil, bound and gagged lay moaning on the floor. They had seen Ricardo come through a narrow opening in the opposite side of the grotto and kick the helpless boy. Now he was running up to Pedro. The old man because of his deafness was unaware that Ricardo was in the room. Frozen with terror, the girls saw him grab the old man, throw him to the ground and beat him into unconsciousness. For a moment, he stood there looking down at his victim and uttering threats, then he started for the idol.

There was no need to tell Judy and Susanne what he was planning to do. They knew he had double-crossed Marie and had come by himself to steal the War God.

Frantic, Judy moved over to the opening, raised her flashlight and with all the strength she could muster, threw it straight at the Indian's dark, handsome face.

Ricardo gave a cry of pain and rage. But be-

---

* AUTHOR'S NOTE. In Carleton Beal's book on Mexico, he writes of the worship of idols by Indians. It is done in secret, and only by old Indians. When I lived in Central America, a mining engineer told me that many times he had seen offerings of flowers and fruit on the shores of lakes. An idol was supposed to have been thrown into these bodies of water. For years the Church has tried to stop the worshipping of idols, but has had little success.

fore he could see who had thrown the flashlight the girls were racing out of the cavern calling wildly for help.

Their seemingly futile call was answered. Like a miracle help was coming. There was the flashing of lights, the shouting of voices, the sound of running feet as down the tunnel came Mr. Stanton, Francisco and two other Indians.

Judy called, "Hurry! Hurry! Pedro's dead. Phil's hurt. Get Ricardo quick! He's in there. He's back in there," she said, pointing to the cave. "Oh hurry, before he gets away!"

It did not take long for the men to overpower Ricardo. The girls crouched against the wall as two men hustled him by them.

They ran back to the grotto, but big, ruddy-faced Mr. Stanton hurried to the opening and barred the way.

While he was talking they could see Phil sitting on the floor his hands and arms unshackled and he was holding his right ankle. Francisco was on his knees beside Pedro trying to ease the old man's suffering. There was a gleam of silver on the table and the two pine torches on either side of the War God was making the little jade idol a shining, glowing thing.

"You mustn't come in," Mr. Stanton was saying gravely. "This is no place for you now. If you want to help, run home and see that two stretchers are sent at once. We'll take care of everything here."

"Is Pedro dead?" Susanne whispered, her frightened eyes on the old man lying so quietly on the floor.

Mr. Stanton shook his head. "No, but he's dying, Susanne. You can't do anything for him, so please go home as I told you."

Susanne was crying as she turned away. Before going Judy had to find out something. She had to know if Pedro had helped Phil steal the idol. She did not mention Phil, but with her eyes filled with tears she asked brokenly, "Pedro didn't have anything to do with stealing the idol, did he, Mr. Stanton? Oh I hope he didn't."

They were startled by a cry from Francisco. He was on his feet looking down at Pedro. "He's dead!" he was crying in Spanish. "*Oh Señor, Pedro's dead! Madre de Dios! Madre de Dios! Pedro's dead.*"

Mr. Stanton said quietly, "Get the stretchers, Judy. You and Susanne hurry and get the stretchers."

CHAPTER XV

EXPLANATIONS AND A WIND STONE

A week later life on the Harrington plantation was going along in its customary manner.

There was a newly made grave in the little Indian cemetery. Although it was the grave of Pedro, a thief, every day Judy and Susanne covered it with flowers.

Pedro had been almost beside himself when he learned that Judy, Phil and others had brought a curse upon them by handling the War God. He carried the idol down to the catacomb in order to appease its wrath with worship and offerings. It was he who stole Susanne's jewelry and the silver goblet and tray, and it was he who gave the War God his gun, his most precious possession.

Rosetta who was now able to sit up confessed that it was Pedro who had shot her. She was with him when he offered his gun to the idol. "The War God was very angry," she said gravely, "for he made Pedro stumble and fall and the gun went off shooting me in the arm."

Marie was heartbroken over what Ricardo had done. She admitted that it was Ricardo who had climbed up to the girls' room and stolen the key.

In her delirium, again and again Rosetta had talked about the monastery, the idol and a secret door. In order to have more opportunity to locate the door and steal the idol Ricardo fixed up the ghost, hoping the girls might become so frightened they would leave. When this did not work he got Marie to send them up river. She was so conscience stricken, so repentant over what she had done and what she had been planning to do, that she was forgiven.

Phil's ankle was badly sprained. Almost dizzy with happiness, he was spending the fragrant, cool days in a steamer chair in the Harrington patio; Judy and Susanne waited upon him as though he were a king.

He told them, "Pedro was sure surprised when I walked into the grotto. He tried to reason with me to let the idol alone, to go home and keep still about it. When he found I wouldn't do such a fool thing what did the old fellow do but tie me up! Once I got away, and was going down the tunnel for all I was worth when I stepped into a hole and sprained my ankle. Oh boy, did it hurt! He brought me back and because I kept hollering for help, stuck a gag in my mouth; only took the darned thing out when he gave me something to eat and drink."

Released from a promise, Phil explained his incriminating actions. "When I was a kid Francisco saved my life," he said, "and ever since then, I've been sort of 'loony' about him. He had been drinking, and when I heard a rumor that someone had climbed up to the girls' room and stolen the key, I was afraid it was our good-for-nothing Francisco."

Phil said he was hoping there was nothing to the report, but when he went over that morning and found it true, he waited until the girls showed him the idol, then told them he couldn't go riding and beat it home to accuse him.

Francisco wasn't there. Phil thought he might have gone up river to relatives. They hadn't seen him, so he kept paddling up river to another village where he knew Francisco visited. There he was. He was drunk and still drinking.

"Whatever Francisco is, he isn't a liar," Phil said. "So I knew he was telling the truth when he swore he hadn't been near this house for a week.

"On the way down we heard the idol had disappeared. How that word got way up there doesn't surprise anyone who knows the jungle. Well anyway, after Francisco made me give my word of honor not to bring him into this he told me that he had a hunch Pedro had taken it. He said he was with Pedro last summer when the old fellow found a small, stone idol along the shore of a lake. One day Francisco discovered the secret door to the catacombs and was prowling around down there when he came across Pedro worshipping this little idol.

"Indians are loyal. They never give one another away, so Francisco had never told this. But he figured now it was different. A valuable idol had been taken. He thought we ought to know that Pedro might be worshipping it down in the catacomb.

"When we arrived home Francisco was too drunk to go with me, so I went to the monastery by myself. Big, gangling Francisco was on one of his big sprees and returned up river. He never knew I was missing until he came back the day he brought Dad to the grotto."

Like everyone, their Aunt Alice was very much broken up over the death of Pedro. "Colonel Thompson is right," she said, "a hundred jade idols aren't worth one hair of dear old Pedro's head. But I wish the Colonel would stop blaming himself for taking the idol to the monastery. It is not his fault Ricardo is nothing less than a devil."

On their way home in August, the girls stopped off in Mexico City to visit the National Museum. As the Colonel, their Aunt Alice and Phil also were eager to see the War God in its permanent home, they accompanied Susanne and Judy that far.

The long gallery of archaeology was filled with large and small idols, stones with strange hieroglyphics and many other interesting objects discovered in ancient ruins. In the center of the room was a black marble pedestal and on it the jade idol.

Phil chuckled, "Look at the old duffer. They've sure given him a prominent place, haven't they."

For a few minutes they stood before it in silence; the Colonel was staring at it with the pride of an archaeologist.

Susanne had not come very close, and as usual, was eyeing it with fear.

Judy was thinking of that early morning in the monastery when Colonel Thompson had shown them the idol. She could see herself later in the day back in the old chapel showing the idol to Phil, then holding the little War God, and standing in a shaft of sunlight for Susanne to take her picture. The next time she saw it was down in the grotto. She remembered how its yellow eyes glittered under the light of the pine torches.

In spite of her protests, she had always been afraid of it. She was afraid of it now. For the hundredth time she was telling herself "It is only a piece of jade, so it can't have any power to hurt you." But she was grateful for a gift from Phil, a silver encircled wind stone she was wearing on a chain. She was grateful too, for Pedro's necklace of stones, and most of all for his prayers.

Phil was patting the idol on its green head and saying, "Hi there, squirt! Glad to see us? Sure you are," he laughed. "Hey girls, look at him grin."

Susanne said in a horrified voice, "Keep your hands off him, Phil! For heaven's sake don't touch him!"

Back of them a guide was talking to a group of tourists. "Ladies and gentlemen, this little War God was brought here only a few weeks ago. Please note it is made of jade, making it a rare specimen. I regret I know nothing of its history. But it is unlikely that anything out of the ordinary is connected with this pretty little idol."

As they moved on Judy drew a long breath. "Nothing out of the ordinary," she was thinking, "Only the death of a man and a curse on all who touch it."

She looked again at the War God sitting on its black pedestal. She looked at the gold snakes twined about its green body, at the necklace of gold hearts and at the idol's fierce, yellow eyes. Never again did she want to see this horrible old thing! She turned away. "Please let's go," she begged. "Please, let's get out of here."